P

I found Firevein: The Awakening to be an emotionally intense and character-driven read. What stood out to me most was the strong focus on relationships — the connections between characters felt passionate and, at times, overwhelming in a way that really pulls you into their world.

— BOOKSIRENS READER

Good golly!! Not only was this so beautifully written, it was, exquisite!! But, the story. THE STORY!! ❤

— LIZ'S BOOKSHELVES

PRAISE FOR HANNA PARK

"I will always love you, from one lifetime to the next."

Well, that was fun and so romantic (and hot!)

A Norwegian hero is such a refreshing (in a scorching way) change. A hero that is MORE than just a human is just plain overkill...

That was a great read. I loved the teasing banter between the two. And my, if a six foot ten sexy giant tells you that if he makes me laugh he'll have t marry me according to ancient lore then it won't take me long to burst into laughter. And he likes to pleasure his woman. And he's sweet. And he's a chef...

— VIRGINIE MARCONATO, AUTHOR

I wish I could visit the worlds Hanna Park brought to life

— BOOKSIRENS READER

FIREVEIN: THE AWAKENING

HANNA PARK

BAISONG PRESS

Firevein: The Awakening

This novel is a work of fiction. Any historical references have been interpreted creatively, and this book is not intended to be a factual or scholarly representation of history or mythology.

All characters, events, and settings are either purely fictional or used fictitiously. Any resemblance to actual persons, living or dead, is entirely coincidental.

Cover Art by *Niki White* www.nikiawhiteart.com

Visit Hanna Park at www.hannapark.ca

Baisong Press, Box 291, Port Carling, ON P0B1J0

This edition published 2026.

Firevein is an expanded novel based on the work originally published as *Unwrapped in Røros* by The Wild Rose Press in 2023.

Digital ISBN; 978-1-0696340-2-3

Paperback ISBN; 978-1-0696340-3-0

Published in Canada

CONTENTS

THE LOST PROPHECY

Four times her flame has failed.
The words were not written once, but many times—
remembered, misremembered,
whispered when the mountain believed itself alone.
On the fourth, the fire beneath her bones wakes.
And the King-Below stirs.
Deep enough that stone does not refuse him.
Deep enough that silence bends.
Should she claim what sleeps inside her,
the binding will split.
One will rise beside her light.
And one will rise because of it.
The prophecy does not name which rising saves.
It never does.

1

THE MAN WITH THE MISMATCHED EYES

C*ristabel*

"Anything to declare?" The customs officer flipped through my passport pages and lifted his head. His droopy face reminded me of my neighbour's hound—nosy and downright mean.

"Me? No." How many times had a security agent stopped me on this trip to Norway?

"Excuse me?" His shoulders tensed as he lowered his chin, his bloodshot eyes tired but sharp.

I stood my ground. I dared not waver.

"You look tired. Long day?" I flashed my brightest smile, tossing this man some sugar.

"Ms. Johnson?" His words were a heavy sigh. "Do you have anything to declare? Answer the question, please."

"I did. Nothing to declare. Nada. Just little old me, living my best life." I lifted my eyelashes, adding an exaggerated exhale for good measure.

I knew exactly what I was doing. If I laughed first, nothing got close enough to hurt.

"The reason for your visit today? Business? Pleasure?" The customs officer blinked once, then twice, as if waking from a bad dream.

"My friend is getting married. On Christmas Eve! Can you believe it? I fucking love that girl." I twirled my finger around the black highlight framing the side of my face and grinned.

"Have a nice holiday, Ms. Johnson." He flipped to page sixteen of my passport, slammed the stamp down, and sent me on my way.

The automatic doors sighed open, cold rushing at me like a living thing. Not just air—*weight* pressing against my cheeks, my throat, my chest. I leaned in, one hand tightening on the handle of my carry-on, moving with the crowd.

Airports all felt the same after a while—fluorescent, recycled, half-forgotten as soon as you left them.

You're tired, I told myself. *You've been travelling too long. Everything feels strange when you're exhausted.* The explanation sounded sensible. I held onto it.

As I stepped forward, the floor shifted—just a breath, enough to make my heart lurch.

Salt touched my tongue. Sharp. Cold.

That was new. I didn't panic—panic wasted energy.

The sensation vanished as quickly as it had come, leaving only a faint pressure in my legs—a flinch, unbidden. My body had tensed as if it remembered how.

Without a backward glance, I rolled my wheeled carry-on, trailing behind a man—the behemoth wearing a sturdy red parka and a yellow-striped beanie, his scent wrapping me in the feathered boughs of a Scots pine.

I didn't look at him right away.

I watched the crowd shifting around him.

I didn't mistake it for romance. Romance was noisy. This was quiet. Like standing near someone who knew how to take up space without demanding it.

Stop it, I thought. *You're projecting.*

My gaze followed him before I could stop it. Once I saw him, the distance between us felt temporary.

Bright pendant lighting—downlights shaped like airplane engines—led tired travellers past alternating yellow and blue pillars. My gaze settled on one of those contoured lounge chairs, anything other than him. I needed sleep—sleep and gum. I ran out of gum during the last layover. I hummed along to the jingle-jangle of holiday tunes drifting through the airport sound system.

"*God Jul! Velkommen*!" A young woman stood in the aisle, greeting arriving passengers at Trondheim. She wore traditional clothing: a snug red vest with silver buttons, her white blouse fastened with a sparkling brooch, and her rich blue double skirts embroidered with snowflakes. She held out a silver tray with disposable shot glasses, each filled to the top with clear liquor.

"This is nice. Aren't you cute? I love your outfit. So festive." Slugging back the offered shot, I swallowed it the wrong way, choking on a hot exhale, coughing up caraway flavours, and tasting black licorice all over again. Heat followed—not sharp, not sudden, but spreading wrong. My chest gripped, then eased, then warmed again, slower this time. The warmth rolled instead of burned.

For half a second, the floor wasn't solid. My stomach tipped sideways, like a boat lifting under a wave. Wood creaked somewhere deep in my ears—not a sound, exactly, but the memory of one.

I inhaled sharply, grounding myself, the airport snapping back into place.

I pressed my palm to my forehead without thinking. Nothing hurt. Nothing raced. The sensation just… *stayed*.

"Woohoo. That's some bad medicine." I wiped my mouth with the back of my hand.

"It's better with a beer chaser." His throaty chuckle shook the ground I walked on.

My ears thundered, and the world spun as I turned, drawn to the soothing bass note of his voice. I found myself gazing into Mountain Man's open jacket and the third-button snap of a red flannel shirt. I lifted my chin upward, a sigh escaping my lips.

Odd-colored eyes stared unblinking—one shining baby blue and one chocolate kiss.

"Oh my God, your eyes are fucking amazing. I had a Siberian husky once with eyes like that." I bowled him over with all the charm of a dancing elephant.

Chiselled face, full lips, gold stubble shadowing a square chin—unshaven, how many days? I smiled into those mismatched eyes.

"I said that, didn't I? Out loud for the world to hear?"

"It's not a problem. What's your name?" His voice hitched, and he blinked—the gentle giant taken aback by me.

"Cristabel. Cristabel Johnson. Have we met before? No, of course not. I'd remember. You're... unforgettable." I might have sent the wrong signal to the man. Oh, dear.

He dipped his chin, tucking his beanie into his coat pocket, letting waves of nut-brown hair spill out. Textured strands topped his head—a stylish fade, shaved close on the sides. A muscle feathered in his jaw, and he smiled.

"I love your hair. So Viking. What do they call you? Ragnar Lothbrok? King Olaf?" I searched for the missing clue, only to realize it was standing right there.

"I am neither a king nor a saint. I am Rurik Andersen from Røros."

The way he said it made my pulse skip. Not because of the words, but because of the certainty behind them. He said it as if it were an answer to a question.

I should have pressed. Something about the way he held himself suggested he'd give me the truth if I asked the right way.

Handsome Man flashed two cheeky dimples and a sparkling smile.

"A beer chaser, huh? Well, all righty, then." Standing in his golden glow, I hugged my candy-pink faux fur vest, rocked by a sudden, unwelcome awareness of the space around me.

"You're partly right. Akvavit means 'water of life' and was once seen as a remedy for many ailments." He lifted his chin, his gaze resting on the pretty girl offering refreshments.

"Sir?" Her head dipped, and she curtsied.

I swear her eyes flashed silver.

"Thanks, much." He selected two shooters from the silver tray and offered me one.

"Oh, okay." I stared at the strong stuff. Before I could think, his cup collided with mine. My breath hitched as the liquid, a sharp spill of heat, leapt our rims as if alive.

"Skål!"

The word lingered between us like smoke on a frosty morning.

He hadn't checked if I was ready.

But he also hadn't assumed I wouldn't be.

He treated me like I was a given, not something frail that needed managing.

"Whoa, what was that for?" I recoiled, my fingers sticky from the spilled Akvavit.

"It's a custom. Combining drinks ensures you're not being poisoned." He made it sound less like trivia and more like a habit. His gaze pinned me, something low and deliberate beneath it.

I stared at the fine lines radiating from his pale, intense eyes—a dream come true, or something I shouldn't touch.

The question hung in my mind.

I chuckled, my thoughts spinning. On my first day in Norway, I learned about ancient customs. The observation amused me more than it should.

"Oh, a medieval drinking hack." I joked back. It was easier than admitting I liked how seriously he took my safety. "How many centuries ago are we talking about? Are you the game night trivia champ? I bet you are."

"How did you find out?" He drained his shot glass, his melodic voice soothing my broken soul.

"Good guess, I suppose. *Skål.*" Throwing back the elixir, I banished the last of the cobwebs, a flame igniting deep in my heart. Who was I to snuff it out?

"Better?" His eyes questioned mine.

"No, but I needed that."

I wanted to run my fingers over his glowing skin, the crazed thought overriding all common sense.

I've always hated common sense.

"What brings you to Norway? To the northland? Where did you come from?" His gaze never left mine.

"Me? I'm from Canada." My stomach fluttered, and not from hunger. My pulse felt wrong, too quick, just off.

I stuck out my hand in an exaggerated chop. "It's nice meeting you, Rurik. You said you're from Røros? That's where I'm headed."

When his hand closed over mine—warm and solid, too familiar for a stranger—a tiny shock skittered up my arm.

The world tipped again. This time, it wasn't just me.

Water slammed against something solid. Not glass—wood. My knees bent before I understood why, my body reacting to something my mind couldn't see.

The sensation faded, leaving my hand curled in his. For a heartbeat, his eyes darkened—as if he'd just recognized someone.

Someone else.

"Cristabel," his voice hesitated, testing the vowels. "It suits you."

The sound of it didn't fade the way a name usually did. It settled, something shifting to make room for it.

I didn't move.

Neither did he.

The terminal kept going—wheels rattling, voices rising and falling.

My chest filled with a breath I couldn't release, stretching to the breaking point, and deciding to stay.

I didn't understand it.

A second name rose, unbidden, in the back of my mind.

Astrid.

I blinked, and the word vanished, leaving only his courteous yet devastating smile and the crush of humanity swirling around us.

"You okay?" he asked.

"Fine," I lied. "Jet lag."

I breathed him in, the light bending around him. The noise of the terminal softened, just for a breath, as if someone had lowered the volume. I inhaled—pine, balsam, something crisp and cold that didn't quite belong in an airport.

I blinked hard. I didn't pull my hand back. I told myself I was curious. That was true. I also told myself that if this went nowhere, I'd walk away clean. I'd done harder things than that.

I should have stepped away.

Some part of me had already decided this was a moment to be lived, not avoided. Curiosity had carried me through worse things.

The sensation lingered—a quiet pull I couldn't name.

2

THE CURSE OF REMEMBERING

R*urik*

"Cristabel."

The air between us stilled.

Names mattered. I had learned that the hard way. Doors opened more easily than they closed.

I wasn't inviting what might answer. So I let it stand alone.

Her name lodged in my chest instead of leaving. I had said it before—not this one—but the sound landed cleanly.

I wanted her closer the way a man wanted breath.

A tightening gathered behind my eyes. A pressure low in my ribs—something old waking and refusing to lie back down.

I held myself still. The instinct to step closer rose sharp and immediate, muscle and memory aligning before thought could interfere. For a split second, my footing faltered, as if the ground had rolled beneath me.

Salt rose sharp at the back of my throat. My knees bent, bracing for motion that didn't exist. Not dizziness. Something older. The pitch of a deck meeting open water. My body yielded without falling, the sensation passing as quickly as it came.

Some bindings lived in muscle and scar. I had waited for her before. Waiting was not the danger. Reaching too soon was.

She waited.

Cristabel's stillness was a choice, stripping away any pretense. Whatever she did next, she would own it. I respected that. I would not misread it. I had known that steadiness once, and had missed it when it was gone.

She shifted her weight, one heel rocking back, the movement subtle enough that most people wouldn't notice. The soft fur of her vest brushed her hip, a brief sweep of warmth against skin beneath the open edge.

I felt the urge to mirror her without meaning to—adjusting my stance, matching the distance she held between us. Too close would have been a claim. Too far would have been a retreat.

Her gaze dropped briefly, not to my face this time but to my hands, as if measuring them. When her eyes returned to mine, something unspoken drew taut between us.

Footsteps passed. Luggage wheels rolled. A child cried somewhere behind us. Overhead lights hummed, bright and indifferent, as if nothing unusual had occurred.

Sound moved, and for half a breath, it wasn't voices and wheels anymore, but the rhythm of oars striking water and breath shared--a deep, measured pull. Effort timed to something larger than the self. It returned as motion, then broke apart.

I anchored myself in the present—tile, glass, voices.

"I love how you say my name—so lyrical." She studied me with butterscotch eyes flecked with molten iron, hard yet soft in a way I remembered. "Do you live in Røros?"

"Røros is my home now." The word waited uneasily, as if it hadn't decided whether it belonged to me. A corner of my mouth lifted, a reflex my body hadn't bothered to warn me about.

"Where'd you come from, Rurik? Don't tell me—the Land of the Giants?" Her eyes caught the light.

"Jotunheim is the land you're thinking of." I let the rest remain unspoken. "But no."

Her expression flickered, amused. I allowed myself a small nod, as if we'd just agreed to leave the strangest part of the conversation alone.

There were older answers I could have offered. I had been many things in many places—builder, guardian, witness—but none of those belonged in an airport terminal with holiday music piping through the speakers.

I turned first. "What brings you to Røros?"

"A wedding. Tiinná Kriysi. Do you know her?"

"Yes." My chin dipped once. "It's a small town. Everyone does."

The trolley cut too close. I shifted, stepping into its path before thinking better of it.

My hand lifted toward her elbow and stopped short, fingers curling back into my palm as I adjusted my stance, angling my shoulder between her and the impact. The reflex came from history. That history had cost me.

That same reflex had saved her once. It had failed her once, too.

Her palms lingered, heat pressing through wool and coat and whatever resolve I'd managed to hold in place.

Her breath slowed, then deepened as if she'd noticed it too.

For a moment, neither of us moved.

I could have closed my hand over hers. The shape was already there. Muscle remembered how easily it would fit. The fact that I noticed—and did nothing—would have amused me, once.

I eased back, letting the contact break, her fingers sliding away with a faint reluctance that I did not imagine.

She studied my face, gauging what I had chosen not to do. Then she laughed, already past the danger.

"Oh geez—you saved me. Thanks. Were you hugging a Christmas tree? You smell fantastic." She pressed her palms briefly to my chest and took a breath.

"Laundry soap," I adjusted my cuff, the lie small enough to pass. Woodsmoke lingered beneath it. Resin. Cold iron. Scents that didn't belong to the city air. I had stopped trying to scrub them away a long time ago.

She accepted the answer because she wanted to.

Something tried to surface—cold air biting skin, wool damp with snow, breath too close in the dark. I shut it down before it sharpened.

"I believe you're staying at my hotel. The Gårdshuset in Røros."

"Did we talk on the phone?" She looked up, her brows creasing.

I closed my hand into a fist and let it open again. "You called to confirm your reservation."

The facts—dates, records, things that could be written down and verified. Mortal things. Bound things.

"Yes! Oh my God, yes." She stepped back, gaze drifting

to shop windows trimmed with garlands and mannequins in snowflake sweaters.

Her reflection slid in and out of the glass as we walked —sometimes doubled, sometimes fractured by light and ornament. Once—only once—I thought I saw someone else there, standing half a step behind her.

Something shifted in the glass and was gone. I didn't look again—looking invited answers.

"How do you know Tiinná?" My mind turned with possibilities, and found none.

"We lived together back in school. Made a wedding pact. I went to hers. She goes to mine." She smiled. "Sounds silly, but here I am."

She slowed near a holiday display—reindeer, a life-sized sleigh, gnomes popping up and down behind mossy stumps—snapped a photo, then turned toward me.

"Do you mind? She won't believe who I ran into at the airport."

Her laughter rang out, bright and unguarded, its sound striking deep.

I did not let it show.

Her happiness made her visible, and visibility demanded care. I scanned the room without turning my head.

She slipped an arm around my waist, her smile lighting her phone's screen, then tucked it away, falling into step beside me as we passed a display of glass ornaments catching the overhead light.

"And did she go to yours?" The question rose, unguarded.

"Nope. She still owes me."

She stopped near the tree, studying an ornament as if it had personally offended her. When she stopped, I stopped.

She glanced back over her shoulder. "Are you coming?"

I stepped closer and let my hand rest at the small of her back—not guiding, not claiming. Just contact. I removed it as soon as she moved again.

An elf cut across our path, bells chiming as he offered slabs of dark chocolate dusted with crushed candy canes. Cristabel halted, eyes lighting.

"Oh—wow. Is that dark chocolate?"

She tasted it, eyes closing, murmuring soft sounds. I kept my attention on the space around her instead of her mouth.

"She's the town doctor." I shifted my weight, watching her instead of the elf. "Everyone's doctor."

She turned toward me, chocolate forgotten, studying my face with that sharp, assessing stillness. "She recommended your hotel. The Gårdshuset. It means farmhouse. Is it still one?"

"It was." I reached for a shopping basket as we entered the duty-free area, placing it in her hands. "A long time ago."

She accepted it without comment, fingers curling around the handle as if it belonged there.

I stopped walking.

She took two steps before noticing and turned back, her brow lifting.

"Do you need a ride, Cristabel?"

"I'm sorry—what?"

"I'm headed that way, to Røros."

Her gaze drifted to the shelves. She caught a dark strand of hair and wound it once around her finger.

I didn't fill the silence.

"That's kind of you." A smile lifted her lips.

Kind would do.

"I'd enjoy the company."

The pause that followed lingered between us—thick with what neither of us intended to say.

Cristabel didn't answer right away. Her gaze drifted past me toward the terminal doors, then back again, mapping distance instead of destination. She adjusted the basket in her hands, fingers tightening briefly around the handle.

When she smiled, it wasn't playful this time. It carried consideration.

"That's tempting." Her fingers tightened on the basket handle, then loosened.

A breath left me, restrained before it became a laugh.

"I can get you safely to Røros." I held her gaze and let the rest remain unsaid.

She shifted her stance, just enough to put space back between us without retreating.

I waited.

3

WHAT THE BODY KNOWS

R*urik*

"Thanks, but as I said, I have a room booked in Trondheim. So, I'm taking the train in the morning." She rocked forward, her expression faltering.

I nodded once. It changed nothing.

The idea of her spending the night in Trondheim—alone, unguarded—met resistance.

Want.

I named it. Naming kept it contained.

I slid my hands into my coat pockets, letting the cold sink through me. Acting too soon brought consequences. Yet, my attention refused to loosen.

The longer she lingered, the harder it became to remain still.

She stood there, bright and unmistakable against the terminal's muted palette—pink fur, white hair, that single dark strand slipping loose again, refusing to be tamed.

The crowd moved the way water moves around a stone it hadn't learned to erode. I had stood in that current before.

The memory rose unbidden—salt wind, ironwood oars biting water, the deck slick beneath my boots as the ship pitched and rose.

Some instincts predated choice. Mine did not hesitate.

"Cristabel." A corner of my mouth lifted before I could stop it. Discipline loosened for a breath.

She looked up, and the simple act of it nearly undid me. Not because of her beauty. Because of what met my gaze in return—recognition, clean and exact, locking into place as if it had always meant to.

I remained where I was, my breath calm. When I spoke, I kept my voice even, polite, and composed.

"If you change your mind." I gave her a slight nod. "I'll be here." I had stood there before. I would again.

Her gaze lingered on my face, searching—not prying, not demanding, just… noticing. As if she felt it too—the way one step could change everything.

The crowd surged. A suitcase clipped my heel. Someone laughed too loud nearby, the world insisting on continuing.

I remained, my feet locked in place, because some things demanded time once they finally returned. I had waited for her before.

Wanting her was not the danger.

Losing her was.

Cristabel

A ride to Røros with a handsome man was a terrible idea—which, historically, had never stopped me before.

I shifted my weight from one foot to the other, the strap of my bag biting into my shoulder as if it were trying to hold me in place. My thoughts scattered, grasping for something solid—anything that wasn't the pull of him beside me.

Vodka felt like the safest decision I could make in that moment. Predictable choices were easier to manage than whatever this was already tugging at me. Familiar. Small. Something I could explain to myself later, if I needed to.

I let the shelves decide for me, my attention snagging on glass and price tags. I examined a price tag, mentally converting the Norwegian kroner to Canadian dollars.

"Buy it here. Everything in town is more expensive." His melodic voice rumbled low, the sound settling deeper than it should. "Consider it airport survival advice," he added, eyes glinting.

I snorted—low, embarrassing—my shoulders dipping, my body deciding something my mouth hadn't caught up with.

"More expensive? Fuck me, that's a lot for a bottle of vodka." I cradled the liquid gold in my arms, something warm and restless pooling low in my chest.

"You've got it." He placed a one-litre bottle in his basket and then walked away.

I watched him longer than was polite. I didn't follow him because that would have felt reckless. Letting him come back felt… different. I didn't chase. I just… didn't leave.

"Okay. Well, I guess I'm it," I swept my hair over my shoulder, letting the aisles swallow me.

I drifted past glass and labels and too many choices, my hands busy while my mind refused to be. Mascara, eyeliner, lip gloss in colours I'd never worn but suddenly wanted—scarlet, wild pink, a purple so deep it bordered on reckless. Shopping soothed me. A little.

I sprayed a sample into the air and walked through it, floral and sharp, wondering what his lips would taste like—and didn't push the thought away.

I glanced down at my boots, then up at him, an image of Rurik dancing in my mind—stacked muscles, sculpted and firm. I tilted my head back, then back a little more when he returned. "How tall are you?"

"The last time I checked, six feet ten inches." His gaze held me frozen in time. "Tiinná didn't tell me you were such a beautiful woman."

"Oh…well, geez. You know how to make a girl blush, don't you? What other charms do you possess?"

"If I make you laugh," his mouth tipped at one corner, "you will have to marry me." His mouth curved, unbothered by the weight of what he'd said.

The words caught. Not because I believed them—but because something waited for an answer.

I paused, my heart fluttering with something I couldn't name.

"Marry you? What? Where did that come from?" My thoughts raced through the last ten minutes. I smiled. Did I laugh? "What are you talking about?"

"An old Norwegian fairy tale." He moved sideways, his arms loose at his sides.

"A fairy tale?" I rested my teeth on my bottom lip and stared right back.

For a blink—just one—a boy stood in the middle aisle, too quiet for the chaos around him, dressed wrong for the airport—gold sash, patterned trousers, boots untouched by scuff or snow.

I blinked once. It was gone.

Rurik was already smiling.

Altitude, I told myself again. Connecting flights did strange things to memory. I refused to build meaning out of a blink.

"Often, the humble peasant boy was the only one in the kingdom who could make the princess laugh."

"So the princess is the prize?" I turned my gaze back to Rurik.

"He is the only one who pleases her. The only man in the kingdom who can make her happy." His voice lowered, and with those fairy tale words, he promised the world.

"Oh, a happily ever after? You, Rurik Andersen, are a romantic." My face spread into a smile, my eyes closing for a split second.

"Hmm, perhaps. How long are you staying in Røros, Cristabel?" He placed his hand gently on my lower back, his touch light.

My breath caught before I could stop it.

"I wish I could have arrived earlier, but I couldn't get away. Work, you know? Tiinná insisted on providing my dress. For the wedding?"

I flashed my phone screen, showing a photo of Tiinná modelling a deep navy, full-length dress with intricate embroidery.

I talked more than usual, my thoughts skidding sideways whenever he looked at me.

"Are you a doctor, like Tiinná?" He paused beside an impulse bin full of gum—stick gum, bubble gum, all kinds of gum—tossing a variety into my basket.

I stared at the gum, then at him. I hadn't realized I wanted it until he did. That should have bothered me. Instead, it felt like relief.

My mouth opened, then closed.

"Me? No. God, no. Not a people person. No, not me. I went into veterinary medicine." I closed my fingers and opened them again.

"You're a vet?" He said it slowly, like it mattered.

I hadn't realized how rare that was until it happened. No one said my work like that. It melted my heart in a way that felt dangerously human. I wasn't ready to interrogate the feeling yet.

"Yep—large animals. Lions, tigers, and bears, watch out!"

"Oh, my!" He turned his head, then chuckled. "Isn't that a tough profession? Handling such large animals?"

"Huh, I'm strong as a bull." I flexed my arms, one at a time, showing off impressive biceps. "I work hard for these babies. Strength training. High-protein diet."

"Not bad at all." He pinched my tense muscle between his thumb and index finger.

I stayed where I was, caught in that moment.

"Hmm… " I shifted my jaw, a habit I couldn't break.

"Did you bring a coat? Something besides this?" He tugged at the faux fur of my sleeveless vest, his attention sharpening.

I stepped sideways, testing the space between us—and finding it mine.

"What? You don't like my outfit?" I ran my hand through the air, unable to ignore the full-body shiver coursing through me.

"You're not dressed for Norway." He opened his hands, his gaze sharpened as he examined my outfit—my pink vest, form-fitting jeans, and high-heeled blue suede boots.

"Have you ever been to Toronto, Rurik? Windy and wet. This? The land of Vikings and trolls? Your Norway? Piece of cake." I snapped my fingers, breaking the spell.

Heat gathered low and insistent, with nowhere sensible to go. I stole a sideways glance at the man.

"I appreciate your concern. I do, but I'm fine, perfectly fine." I meant it. Not because I was invincible—but because his concern didn't suffocate me. I could escape. I could walk away. I dug my fingernails into my palms, steadying myself.

He spoke fluent Norwegian to the cashier in the next aisle—the sight of him took my breath away.

I thought of Tiinná then—the way she'd smiled when she told me to pack warm—and decided not to chase the thought.

"I'm sorry, miss. Did you say something?" The cashier's cheerful smile brought me back to the present.

"Um, no. I don't think so." The last thing my friend said—something about fairy tales and Christmas magic. Go figure.

"I'll need your Passport and your boarding pass," she asked, scanning each item and placing them into a bright yellow duty-free bag. "And how will you be paying?"

I looked past her, my mind elsewhere.

Two wooden trolls, tiny miniature beings with big heads and long noses, sat beside a bowl of peppermints—one with wild white hair standing straight up, the other with a crooked grin and long pointed ears. Ridiculous. Familiar.

One of them tipped slightly when I touched it, rocking once. I noticed—and decided not to ask why.

"This one looks like you." Rurik picked up the wild-haired one and held it between us.

"A troll?" I looked at him, my mouth falling open.

"The resemblance is uncanny." He turned the toy troll so its frizzy hair ruffled, his one eye turning a gentle glacier-blue. "It's a compliment. Trolls are lucky, protective, and fierce when needed."

"Really?" I crossed my arms. "So I remind you of… a lucky, protective creature with questionable grooming?"

"Exactly." His lips twitched.

A laugh spilled out before I could stop it. God, it felt good to laugh. "And I'll take the trolls."

Both of them.

"For luck?" Rurik's eyebrows raised, a muscle twitching in his cheek.

"For my friend," I lied. "And maybe for me, too."

"Good choice. Every traveller should carry a little magic." His fingertips brushed mine as he reached for the trolls, placing each on the counter.

Even the trolls seemed to grin wider.

"Miss?" The cashier wrapped each troll in tissue and placed them in the bag.

"Credit, thank you." I tapped the right piece of plastic. When I looked up, Rurik stood in front of the exit.

"Are you sure I can't change your mind? Your room at the Gårdshuset will be ready." The sparkle in his eyes revealed one thing, while the deep resonance of his voice hinted at something else.

His expression tightened, lines fanning from his beautiful eyes.

"Ready and waiting, huh?" I wasn't deciding based on logic. Logic would have sent me in the other direction.

I stared through the revolving glass doors toward the shuttle bus, its destination flashing insistently, the exhaust curling into the cold air like a warning.

My reflection stared back, eyes too bright, cheeks flushed, as if I'd already stepped over something without noticing.

"I can have you in Røros in a couple of hours. No overnight stay. No train ride. And don't forget the great company," his eyes held me like a hand on my back. Then, he shrugged off his parka and handed it to me. "Here, take this."

I grinned, too big, too fast.

"What? No, I'm fine." I patted my rollie bag and smiled at his friendly face. Too friendly?

"You have a coat? In there?" His eyes widened, his voice disbelieving.

"Yes, I do." I tore my gaze from his and fiddled with the zipper, slipping my hand inside the tightly packed space to find what I was after—a packable pink pouch. With a quick tug, the jacket puffed out into a candy-pink ball. I shoved my hands into the pockets, twirling around to show off. "What do you think?"

The bus driver honked his horn, demanding attention.

"Hmm…not bad, but do you have a hat?" He pinched the still-expanding down.

There was something about the way he moved. Was it his eyes? The deep rumble of his voice?

Desire hit, sudden and disorienting. I widened my stance until the world stopped pitching again.

My brows furrowed. I shook my head. "I didn't see you on the flight." I grasped for something ordinary. "Did you connect in Copenhagen?"

"No. I came in from Oslo this morning. Short hop."

"Oh." The simplicity of the answer calmed me more than it should have.

He studied my face for a moment, then his expression softened. "You look cold."

His hand found mine—not urgent, not claiming—just enough. "Let me get you something warm. Coffee. Tea."

That landed—more than I expected. He wasn't asking for anything. Not answers. Not confessions.

No promises.

The urge to stay pressed in, tempting and unreasonable, but clarity finally broke through. I eased my hand free with a quiet laugh.

"A drink?" I grinned. "Hmm… right now, I think you should put your jacket back on before you freeze to death. This is Norway, after all—land of the midnight sun, Vikings, and questionable survival choices."

"I forget sometimes." He adjusted his stance. "I'm used to the cold."

With one finger, he lifted the dark strand of hair and tucked it behind my ear. The simple touch unmoored me more than the dizziness had.

My lips parted.

"I'll take you up on your ride." I surprised myself with how even my voice sounded. "If your offer stands."

"You won't be disappointed." He guided me aside as the shuttle pulled away. "I promise."

I watched the exhaust thin into the cold and realized I was done hesitating. When Rurik's hand settled at my elbow—warm and certain—I didn't pull away. I trusted myself to know the difference.

4

STARS ON THE ROOFTOP

R*urik*

The elevator doors creaked open onto the rooftop of the airport garage. Cold rushed in, carrying the metallic scent of snow and fuel.

I stepped out first, scanning the rows of parked vehicles and the open sky above them—ink-black, scattered with stars burning hard and bright. The wind tugged at my coat, insistent and familiar. I welcomed it. Cold clarified.

Behind me, her footsteps scraped softly across the frozen asphalt—unsteady, distracted. I didn't turn, but my awareness tracked her, the way it always had. The space she occupied shifted when she drew near.

"Look at the stars. How fucking awesome is that?"

She bounced her suitcase over the frozen ruts without looking where she stepped, distracted by the stars, by the open sky, by careless joy. Her foot slid out from under her. A sharp intake of breath cut the air as her arms flung wide, instinct scrambling for balance.

I moved before I thought, the world narrowing to the simple need to stop her from falling. My hand closed around her fingers, momentum carrying her the rest of the way, twisting her neatly into me. Her back settled against my chest.

She fit. Not comfortably. Correctly.

Relief hit first. Then want—sharp and immediate.

The instinct rose—to let my arms tighten, to lower my chin, to breathe her in fully—and my body remembered restraint. I counted heartbeats instead. One for her. One for me. I did not smile.

Then I let go.

She bounced off and finished with a quick two-step. "I was a figure skater in my last life."

"Your last life?" I repeated, stepping back a pace. I treated it as humour because acknowledging it as anything else would have required honesty.

The words last life slid under my ribs, sharp as a blade turned sideways. I had heard them spoken in jest before. From her, they carried weight. She spoke without reaching, and that unsettled me more than belief ever could.

She had come to me in fragments before—never clearly, never whole. Just enough to wake me.

"Um, Rurik… are you okay? You look like you've seen a ghost."

I forced a smile, the practiced kind, and nodded once.

She was real. Sitting beside me. Breathing, laughing, and warm.

"It's going to snow, don't you think?" Her breath frosted as she looked around, sniffing the cold air.

For a split second, my knees bent for a tide that never came. The ground felt unreliable—not gone, just there.

I locked my knees, forcing the sensation back where it belonged. I did not owe the past my attention.

"Yes, a storm is coming. Let me carry your bag." I reached for something ordinary.

I adjusted my grip on her bag, grounding myself in its simple weight. I ignored the tension beneath my ribs.

I noticed her boots then—sharp, elegant things wholly unsuited to ice and distance, made for places where the ground could be trusted. The way she stood in them, weight tipped forward without fear, told me she trusted the ground to behave.

"How do you walk in those?"

The question slipped out before I could stop it—curiosity, not judgment.

"Hey. These are Valentino's. I got them on sale. Retail therapy? Have you heard of it?" She scrunched her shoulders, a shiver running through her, teeth chattering. "Do you always park on the roof? It's fucking cold up here."

"Do you always say 'fuck'?" I blurted out the first thing that came to mind, the corner of my mouth lifting despite myself.

"Hmmm, I guess I do. Do you have a problem with that?" She blew a kiss over her fingertips.

"No. Not a problem. I find it endearing." I lifted her suitcase by the handle, taking ownership of her bag.

"Endearing? What planet do you hail from, Rurik Andersen? Do you ever talk dirty?" She examined me with furrowed brows, her pink lips tinged with blue. Then she huffed and tugged at her zipper. "Good thing I brought my long johns, eh?"

"Would you like my hat?" I offered my toque as a peace offering.

"Your hat? Didn't your mother ever tell you about head lice?" She ran her pink stiletto nails through her wild hair.

"Oh—sorry. I didn't mean to pry." She stopped, her smile softening. "That came out wrong."

She felt the boundary as soon as she crossed it.

"My mother?" The word felt oddly foreign on my tongue. I cleared my throat. "She lives further north."

Distance had always been my most reliable inheritance. It was true.

She accepted the answer without probing. I let that stand.

I led her toward the far end of the lot, my hand hooked over her elbow.

"Here we are. This is my truck."

She assessed.

"Huh, I saw you as an SUV type."

"Why is that?" I stored her carry-on inside the covered box, measuring her reaction.

"How about Norwegian roads? Snow? Better traction?" She hugged herself, uncertainty flickering in her eyes.

Two presses of the release button unlocked the doors. I activated the remote start.

"Okay, wait a moment. How did you manage that?" Her hands pushed through her coat sleeves, brushing the copper accents on the side panels. Then she rested both hands on the passenger window. "Bucket seats?" She looked towards the front of the truck, slipped her hand under the hood, unfastened the catch with practiced ease, and lifted the hood. "This is the eliminator e-crate motor. But this is a Ford F-100, a '78, right? How is that possible? Did you build this?"

"Building trucks is a hobby."

"A hobby? This is fucking amazing." Her voice rose high, then low. She dropped the hood and swore under her breath. "Shit, I broke a nail." She studied her index finger.

"Are you hurt?" I took her injured hand in mine, touch complicating restraint.

"This is not the day I die. Well, at least I hope not. Do you know where I can get my nails fixed?" Her eyes shot fiery darts, her words struck something old.

"Hmm…perhaps Tiinná can advise you on that front." A memory flickered—dark hair, a bowed head, hands steady with focus. I pushed it aside before it could sharpen into anything more.

I held the door open and waited until she was settled into the passenger seat and safely buckled.

"Hmm, not to worry. I have a nail file somewhere." She rummaged through her bag.

"How did you learn so much about trucks?" I gave her the version that ended questions.

As the truck eased into motion, the vibration through the steering wheel deepened—then levelled. Shifting gears, I followed the circular ramp down to ground level.

"Worked my way through school by swinging wrenches. For my uncle?"

She spoke of engines the way others spoke of animals—listening first, understanding by feel rather than instruction.

I remembered her hands stained with ink. Head bent.

Focus absolute.

I did not follow the memory further.

"Hmm. How curious. And what kind of vehicle do you

drive?" As the truck rolled forward and the stars slipped behind us, I kept my attention on the road—on motion instead of memory.

5

THE KISS THAT REMEMBERS

R*urik*

"Me? A full-size pickup. Hot pink." Her lips pinched crookedly before she smiled.

"You drive a pink truck?" I laughed before I could stop myself.

"Yes—why? Is that funny?" She tipped her head, hair swinging loose around her face, eyes bright and searching.

I guided the truck onto the highway, Trondheim shrinking in the rearview mirror, the road ahead dark and narrowing.

She studied me. "You looked at me like you… knew me."

"I think I gave you the wrong impression earlier. Can we try again? I'm Rurik from Røros. I'm a chef. I own the Gårdshuset Hotel. Sometimes I build trucks." I offered her the parts of myself that cost nothing.

"That's all?" She lifted one eyebrow.

It wasn't all. It was what I could give.

"Yes, that's it."

"Hmm… " She leaned back in her seat, resting her head on the headrest.

"Your turn." One hand stayed on the wheel, the other loose at my side.

"What did Tiinná tell you?" She closed her eyes, shifting her jaw back and forth.

"Nothing about you," I met her gaze. "I didn't know you before today."

The lie was clean.

"You're funny, Rurik. Okay. I'm just Cristabel, veterinarian extraordinaire." She hugged her chest, snuggling into her puffy coat.

"Is there someone waiting for you back in Canada?" I asked the question that mattered most. If there had been, I would have stepped back. Want did not excuse trespass.

"Nope, no ring on this finger." She flipped her fingers into the air. "I might stay a while. At least until after the holidays. I don't have much to go back to."

"Why is that?" Overriding the automated sensors, I set the heat to its maximum for her benefit. Caring was safer than touching.

"Trouble in paradise, I guess." Her stoic expression revealed nothing.

"Work-related, then?" I asked, adjusting the fans as snow began to thicken against the windshield.

She considered the question, fingers laced together. "Not family. I have plenty of those. Loud, loving, complicated. But work?" She exhaled through her nose. "That turned out to be something else entirely."

I heard something tired beneath the words. I didn't press.

"Yeah, who knew, right? Big-box veterinarians…not

what I imagined when I threw my black cap in the air. When I was a kid, I loved the James Herriot books—old-fashioned veterinary medicine. Mr. Herriot would wander the hills and dales in an old jalopy. It's not like that today. Not anymore. Do you read books?"

I let the conversation drift.

"I prefer non-fiction, how-to books." I glanced sideways, wondering where this conversation was headed.

"Oh, a seeker of knowledge. Nothing wrong with that." She craned her neck back and forth, stretching.

My mouth went dry at the thought of her skin there—warm, unguarded. I forced my attention back to the road.

"And what about you? What makes Cristabel Johnson smile?" I slowed the truck, expecting the upcoming bend in the road.

"Oh, not much. I still love my work." She gazed into the swirling white fury. "From now on, though, I'm living in a world of whimsy. I've made up my mind, and I won't be going back." She raised her hand, twirling the silky black locks between her fingers.

"So, I'm not the only romantic." I glanced sideways.

"Maybe I am. I'm here, after all—for Tiinná and her holiday wedding." She gave me the sweetest smile, with a hint of laughter. "How are you spending the holidays?"

"Me? The hotel is packed with travellers." The wipers scraped the glass, leaving frozen white streaks. I opened the window, filling the cab with winter's cold breath.

"Busy with work, huh? Okay. Are you married?" She studied me, her questioning gaze distracting me from my task.

"Not yet." I made a one-handed catch of the swishing rubber, letting the wiper fall and dislodging the ice pack.

"Not yet? Oh, I see. Do you play this game with all the girls?" She shrugged her shoulders, giving me a curious smile.

"Once in every lifetime." I smiled as if it were a joke. It wasn't.

The word lifetime felt older than the road beneath the tires.

"Once in every lifetime? You're really killing it with this fairy tale thing." Her teasing voice sent chills racing through my bones, but then she went quiet, as if something had caught in her chest.

"Do you have plans for Christmas Eve?" Pressing on the console, I selected a holiday playlist.

"Why? Are you asking me out?" She lifted her chin, her eyes gleaming.

"May I accompany you to Tiinná's wedding?" The question caught in my throat.

"The wedding?" She rested her chin on her hand, staring me down with those same eyes, the ones that stole my soul every time. "Okay, I'd love to go to Tiinná's wedding with you."

"Super." I nodded, catching her in a sideways glance. "Are you hungry? There's a diner up ahead." I suggested a stop, hoping she would say yes.

"A diner? Sure, I love diners." She turned in her seat, a soft light in her eyes.

"I know."

My grip tightened on the wheel.

"What do you know, Rurik?" Her lips curved into a smile.

"You like pink. You don't like Akvavit. You tense in

crowds. You smell like soap when you've just come out of a bath." I shared small tidbits of the one I loved.

"Who are you? How do you know that?" Her gaze burned into mine.

"Lucky guesses. I pay attention."

"Mind-reading? Hmm." She placed her palms on her knees. "Okay, this is too weird. There's something—an attraction—and it's not jet lag. What is it?"

She was closer than she realized.

"My irresistible charm?" I glanced sideways, noticing her brow furrowed and her lips pressed into a tight line.

"No, more like déjà vu. Like I've been here before. Let's get back to this lightning between us?" She smiled, then smiled again.

"Careful." I grinned. "At this rate, I'll end up owing you snow angels and hot chocolate before we even reach Røros."

Her scent. Her proximity. Everything about her tightened something I had kept leashed.

"Do you think we should stop? There's so much snow. I can hardly see where we're going."

Snow battered the windshield. The lane lines vanished.

She shivered once, small and involuntary, and something inside me snapped loose.

I eased the truck onto the shoulder, my pulse quickening.

She turned toward me, her lips parted as if she were about to speak. Something tight and familiar pulled taut. I hesitated once. Then I leaned in.

"What are we doing?" Her whisper was soft and teasing.

"You're trembling." I ran my thumb over hers.

"That's because it's cold." Her voice lifted. She licked her lips.

Her gaze drifted to my mouth and lingered there—long enough to land.

I didn't move. Not yet.

I waited, close enough to feel the warmth of her breath, close enough that stepping back would have been a lie. My hand tightened once at my side, the effort of stillness straining every nerve.

"Cristabel…" Her name left me rougher than I intended.

She tilted her chin, just slightly, as if answering something she hadn't asked out loud.

She leaned in—soft and sure—her breath breaking as her fingers curled into my coat.

I kissed her slowly. Not taking. Not claiming. I took my time.

Heat surged—sharp and immediate—burning through the restraint I had kept. When her tongue brushed mine, I lost what little distance I'd held onto.

My hand slid to the back of her head, fingers threading into her hair, holding her there—not hard, not claiming—just enough to feel her answer.

I caught her lower lip gently between my teeth, coaxing a soft sound from her before I forced myself to ease back.

Her eyes were wide when I did—dazed, unguarded—like she'd forgotten where we were, and didn't yet care.

"What—what was that?" she whispered.

"The beginning." I brushed her cheek with the back of my knuckle.

"But… we don't know each other." Her breath shook.

"We know enough—for tonight."

She blinked, unsure what to do with that information

"Let's stop at that diner."

She laughed again, softer this time. Her laughter brought me back.

I didn't kiss her again. If I had, I wouldn't have stopped.

"You're safe with me."

The world outside grew silent—snow, moonlight, and nothing else—yet she lit the cab like a torch in the dark.

She studied my face, then nodded once. "Okay, but I still can't see a thing." Her lips shone, her voice low and smoky.

I pulled into the parking lot, guided by the glow of light from the rectangular windows of the roadside diner, the neon sign blinking *open* in crimson red.

She pressed her forehead to the window, breath fogging the glass. "There are no stars—just white snow on white snow. Maybe I do need that hat."

"I hope you're hungry. The diner makes a great *kveldsmat*."

6

A TOWN MADE OF WINTER LIGHT

R*urik*

"Coffee was never going to be enough. You deserve real Norwegian food." My gaze stayed on the diner windows.

"You're full of upgrades tonight." Her sideways glance lingered. "First the ride. Now a feast?"

"There are four meals here." My tone stayed easy. "Breakfast, lunch, dinner… and *kveldsmat*—the fourth meal. Almost like breakfast, but better. Something you eat when the night runs long, and no one's ready to call it over."

The diner windows glowed against the storm, amber and unwavering, the kind of light that made promises it couldn't keep.

"Oh, I would have been happy with a burger, but hey, an all-day breakfast? I'm in."

By the time my feet hit the pavement, Cristabel had already dashed ahead and waited at the front door.

"After you, sir." She held the door open and pointed to the sign that read, "Seat Yourself."

"How's this?" I placed my hand on her lower back and guided her toward a booth.

She slowed half a step instead of moving away. I gazed into her eyes, my thumb resting there a fraction too long before I let her go.

She shrugged out of her coat, draping it over the vinyl seat beside her, cheeks pink from the warmth. I followed suit, hanging mine on the back of the booth.

"Lovely." She sat down, resting her elbows on the table, her gaze wandering over the empty diner.

I slid across from her, reaching for the menu.

"It's nice and warm here." She stretched her fingers toward the heaters humming softly beneath the table.

When she tucked one foot beneath the other, her boots nudged the base of the booth. The table shifted slightly with the movement.

"It's usually busy." I angled my knees so we weren't quite touching—but close enough that the heat of her leg bled through denim.

A server stepped out of the kitchen, greeting us with a curtsy and a friendly nod. Moments later, returning with cutlery for the table, leaving a glass bottle of tap water flavoured with sliced cucumber.

"This is nice. Thank you." Cristabel filled my water glass, then her own. "I love these." She focused her attention on the jukebox, turning the selection knob and then pressing the buttons to choose a familiar tune.

"The pleasure is mine." I clinked my glass against hers. "To us." I didn't look away when I said it.

I watched her fingers curl around the glass, the way she smiled as if she liked the sound of it.

Cristabel leaned in, unafraid of what might answer. "Do you want to splash drinks again?" She peered through a fringe of snow-white lashes, her eyes resting on mine.

"I believe we're safe. If not, I'll consider it a very good way to go."

"Are you always this charming?" Her brows lifted.

"You think I'm charming?" I held back the urge to touch her, to draw her closer again.

Before she could answer, the server returned, balancing two wooden boards and a ceramic platter. She set them down with practiced ease—dark bread stacked thick and warm, small bowls arranged like offerings: pink cod roe, pickled herring, cured elk sausage, smoked mackerel in red sauce.

"Wow," Cristabel breathed. "You weren't kidding."

Her eyes stayed on the spread as she spun the wooden turntable, taking it all in. She lifted a ceramic spoon, drizzling spirals of black bee honey into the pot, then reached for a jar of blackcurrant jelly.

"Would you like tea? Or milk?" I asked as the server added the final platter: sliced egg, tomato, and cucumber—a feast prepared for the hungry.

"I haven't had milk since I was a little girl. Okay, a glass of milk, please." She sampled the Norwegian brown cheese with hesitation and then with eager enthusiasm.

She tasted each thing as if it mattered, as if food wasn't fuel but a story. She ate like she expected joy.

"Try this." I prepared an open-faced feast full of flavour, and I offered her a taste.

"Hmm…yum. Do you do this every night?" She looked up.

"Most evenings." I watched, captivated, as she nibbled from the outside edges inward until nothing was left, then dabbed her mouth with a white napkin.

When she smiled, the storm felt far away.

"Look at this satellite imaging. This snowstorm isn't letting up." She pointed at the weather app on her smartphone. "Should we get a room, Rurik?"

A roadside room. Warm. Anonymous.

I went quiet and studied the table.

"A room?" I let my gaze linger on her lips. "Are you asking me to stay?"

"I was hoping for that happily ever after moment, the kind you read about in steamy romance novels…" Scooting toward the edge of her seat, she placed her hand over mine, her thumb tracing the inside of my wrist—slow, unhurried. Testing. Her voice teased, and her eyes glowed golden. "We'd agree to sleep in the same bed, and when I returned, you'd pretend you're asleep, but…why are you looking like that?"

"Do you read many romance novels?" I stilled.

"I do. Yes, romance makes me hot—for BOB." She widened her eyes, giving me a playful grin.

"Bob?" My voice slipped lower than intended.

"BOB…b.o.b.—battery-operated boyfriend?" She laughed, batting my arm with her broken fingernails. "Let me go fix my face, huh? I'll be right back."

She slid out of the booth and disappeared toward the restroom, boots clicking once before the door swung shut.

I stayed where I was. Let my hands rest on the table until the surge passed. Beyond the counter, keys hung in neat rows behind the desk, tagged and numbered, swaying faintly whenever the door opened.

I looked away.

When she returned, cheeks flushed and hair smoothed back into place, I stood without thinking. We reached for our coats at the same time. Our fingers brushed once, then retreated.

I left enough euros on the table to cover the bill.

"You're not going to let me pay my share, are you?" She clasped my wrist, her eyes questioning.

"My treat, Cristabel." I guided her toward the reception.

"Thanks, Rurik. That was amazing." She stood on her tiptoes, planting a quick kiss on my cheek.

The bell over the door chimed as we stepped outside, the cold reclaiming us, snow falling thick and steady.

"Wow, this storm is in no hurry to loosen its grip, is it?" She hugged her arms around her chest, the wind pushing her toward the truck.

"Tomorrow should be clear and cold. No snow." I opened her door, closing it softly as she settled in.

The rest of the drive was quiet. Conversation thinned as the road stretched on, snow softening the world into a tunnel of white. She drifted in sleep, with her head resting on my shoulder. I adjusted my grip on the wheel without shifting. Her breathing fell into rhythm with the tires, slow and even, and for a stretch of kilometres the world narrowed to movement and stillness.

I slowed at the edge of town, the tires whispering over packed snow.

I lifted my hand and brushed my knuckles lightly against her sleeve. Just enough.

"Cristabel," her name slipped from my lips.

She stirred, drew a breath, then straightened, blinking as she pulled herself upright. Her hair fell loose across her cheek as she found her bearings, one hand braced on the seat between us.

"Welcome to Røros." I gestured toward the lights cresting the hill.

"Oh my God," she whispered, already turning toward the window. "You live in a Christmas card."

Her gaze flicked from the snow-lit eaves to me, undecided where to land. Then she rolled down the window, letting the cold rush in.

Seeing it reflected in her face made the cold feel earned.

She laughed, leaning forward to take it all in—wood-framed buildings, garlands strung low, ice candles burning at every threshold.

As we drove through the narrow street toward the inn, lantern light spilled across the snow in soft amber pools. Curtains shifted and stilled. A man paused mid-step outside the apothecary, then continued on. A door closed a fraction too late.

Nothing she would question. Not yet.

But I felt the pressure under stone and timber before the truck even turned the corner. The old current that runs under stone and timber turned once, testing.

Curious.

My hands stayed steady on the wheel.

She is not yours to measure.

The current eased—but it did not retreat.

"Here we are. Home."

7

THE HOUSE THAT WAITS

R*urik*

"Yes, here we are." She looked at the old hotel and offered me an inquisitive smile.

The house took her in all at once. It always knew when something returned.

I sensed it before I saw it—the way the air seemed to listen, the way the old beams eased into themselves. The Gårdshuset had survived wars and winters that bent men. It knew the difference.

Cristabel smiled, unaware of what had stirred.

"Let me help you." I climbed out of the truck, opened the passenger door, and offered my hand.

"My, aren't you the knight in shining armour?" She slid down, her gaze drawn to the centuries-old inn—the one I had owned for longer than most people could imagine.

The dark-pitched logs were fitted together, rising two stories high, with the mullioned windows overlooking the courtyard, the thatch-covered roof topped with a thick blanket of snow. Trees that learned to grow crooked under snow made the strongest walls. The house wore its age without apology. It didn't shine. It waited.

"Look at those windows. Tell me there's a ghost. There has to be a ghost."

"The hotel was built in the eighteenth century," I hesitated long enough to choose my words. "And yes—there is something that lives here. Her name is Mare."

"Mare?" Cristabel blinked. "Like… a horse?"

"No," I grinned. "Like the thing that sits on your chest while you sleep."

Her smile wavered before she laughed it off. That pause mattered. She chose to move forward rather than ask why.

I lingered a beat too long, but she left me, moving toward the four kick-sleds waiting near the entrance.

"What are these?" She reached for a wooden handle.

"Kick-sleds. Guests can use them to get around town when the snow sets in." I motioned toward town. Winters like this had a way of stirring old habits—laughter on the ice, the scrape of runners, breath burning clean in the lungs.

I turned to lift her bag before the memory settled into anything more than weather.

A howling screech emerged from the shadows, and then a yellow ball of raised fur sprinted to a sudden halt right before her feet.

The house answered with a soft creak somewhere above us.

"Oh my God, is that a cat?" She dropped onto her heels and examined the yellow beast who called me his own.

Her grin took my breath away.

Odin had always known. He chose people the way storms chose valleys.

"That's Odin, we call him the ruler of Heaven and Earth," I smirked as I walked toward the door.

"Odin? The Viking god? He's so big. Is he part lynx?" She picked up the cat from the ground, holding him up by his armpits. "Is he yours? Oh my God, what does he weigh? What happened to his eye? Is he blind?"

"He came that way. One blue eye. I can't believe he's letting you do that." I turned, glancing over my shoulder.

"Do what?" She kissed the side of Odin's face, cuddling his long body to hers.

"Hold him like that, with his man parts hanging in the air." I grinned at her, at the cat.

"He's fully intact. Why don't you get him fixed?" She lifted him, examining him as a veterinarian would. When she placed him on the ground, he chirped and wound around her legs.

"Guys don't do that to other guys." I couldn't stop the smile.

Odin chirped again, pleased with himself, tail flicking like a punctuation mark.

I opened the door and stepped aside as she walked into the foyer of the Gårdshuset Hotel. I nodded toward the cloakroom just off the lobby. "You can leave your coat here and your boots there if you wish."

"This is nice. The pictures don't do it justice. What's that odour?" Cristabel shrugged out of her pink coat. With a heavy sigh, she sat on the pine bench, removing her boots.

"The fireplace?" I looked beyond the overstuffed sofas to the stone fireplace, reaching up to the rafters. Hardwood logs glowed in an open hearth. One burst into a fiery spray of red embers.

"No." She shook her head, her gaze thoughtful as she moved across the room, fingers brushing over the many antique pieces—an old desk, an ornately carved sideboard, an armoire.

Beneath her feet, a circular rug—hand-knotted threads of red, purple, brown, and salmon pink. Someone long gone had chosen those colours with care.

I didn't press.

"No, that's not it. Although the fireplace is lovely." She held her palms in front of the blazing fire, her eyes closing. "Whatever it is, the aroma is amazing."

It wasn't just dinner. Old houses kept stories in their walls—smoke, sap, wool, iron.

She turned away, sinking into a leather armchair, grazing the worn brass grommets with her fingers.

"Hmm…yes. Tonight's dinner—Finnbiff, served every Wednesday." The past blurred with the present. My chest hitched.

"Finnbiff?" She lifted her chin, her brows furrowing.

"Reindeer sautéed with bacon, wild mushrooms, and lingonberries. The berries add a wonderful earthy flavour. Ah, but the secret is the brunost. Sweet on the nose. Always a crowd-pleaser." I recapped the ingredients carefully.

"Reindeer?" She tapped her fingers on the armrests, her brows creased.

"Hmm. We have a thriving lichen colony growing

behind the drive shed. The berries become much sweeter if left to ripen on the branch throughout the winter months. It's a tough little plant."

"Lingonberry?" She looked up.

Did she remember?

"Always better the second time around."

I turned away from her gaze, stoking the fire.

"Yes, so many things are."

Fatigue softened her edges, stripped away the careful brightness she used like armour. This version of Cristabel —the unguarded one—was the hardest to look away from.

"But no, no, thanks. I couldn't eat another thing." Her hair swung sideways, resting on her shoulder.

Odin jumped onto her lap, head-butting her chin with a pleased rumble. Guardians did not choose lightly.

"Are you the all-seeing god of the Aesir? Is that why you're called Odin?" She scratched behind his ears, utterly at ease. "I wonder how many little Odins are running around Røros. Huh, big boy?"

Her laugh was playful. Her words struck too close to something I didn't want named. I swallowed, holding the reaction still.

"I'll leave you two alone for a moment. I'll be right back." I dipped my head and forced myself toward the foyer, pretending I didn't feel the tug of that ancient thread between us.

"No hurry—we're good." She glanced up at me, smiling as she stroked the length of Odin's back, utterly unaware of what had woken.

Odin's meow was a series of chirping screeches.

"Well, aren't you the cup of drama?" she murmured as

she ran her palms over his furry head, her voice reverberating through the room.

I woke the computer screen behind the reception desk and checked the reservation for Cristabel Johnson, who was staying for three nights. Econo single. The thought of her sleeping in the barest of accommodations didn't sit well. Not generosity. Restoration. The house preferred things in their proper place. I searched the reception drawer for the spare key to my suite, the one I had slept in for an eternity of nights. When I returned, I found her nodding off, her eyelashes resting on her pale cheeks, her pouty lips half-parted, with Odin sitting beside her, his paw carefully resting on her knee.

"Cristabel?" I rested my hand on her shoulder.

"Oh, hello." She jumped up from the chair, Odin landing on the floor with a heavy thud.

"Your suite is down here." I led her across the patterned carpet and down a long hallway. "There's a bathroom on the right and a sitting room on the left." I unlocked the door and handed her the key.

"I didn't book this. I booked a Euro room with a twin bed."

"I upgraded you. The storm's not finished. I wanted you somewhere more comfortable. Quieter." I held her gaze. "You deserve that."

I stepped back half a pace.

"If you'd rather have what you reserved, I'll change it."

She stilled, taking in the sitting room, the oversized bed beyond the archway, the heavy drapes.

"You upgraded me," she repeated—quieter this time.

Odin slipped past, leapt to the windowsill, and disappeared behind the blackout curtain.

"Oh—do you want Odin back?" She crossed to the window and pulled the curtain aside, peering beyond the shadows into an endless forest of birch and pine.

She paused.

"Strange," she whispered, more to herself than to me.

I fought the urge to step closer.

"He can stay." I motioned toward the cat.

Odin's tail thumped once in agreement, already settled. Some guardians chose their posts quietly. I envied that certainty.

"What about you, Rurik? Will you stay? For a night-cap?" Her gaze moved over the wine cooler filled with vintage wines, and then back to me.

"I have something else in mind. Something very Norwegian. How about I surprise you?" I held her gaze.

"I love surprises." She padded back to me, placing her hands on my shoulders and pressing a quick kiss to the side of my face. Her fingers lingered at my collarbone a fraction longer than necessary.

Her lips were alive against my skin. I remembered the way that warmth had deepened under my mouth. The contact lingered long after she stepped away.

"Great. I'll be back in a moment." I smiled and softly closed the door.

Staying would have been easier. Leaving was necessary. I forced myself toward the corridor instead, pressing the wanting down into the same quiet place I keep other dangerous things.

This Cristabel joked her way through fear. Glacier on the surface. Fire underneath.

The mountain has a habit of noticing heat.

A cold prickle slid up my spine.

I glanced over my shoulder, half-expecting Ingrid to appear and scold me for serving gløgg too soon. Ingrid had a talent for appearing when rules were bent, and I had broken most of them already.

The simmering pot of mulled wine hissed softly, cinnamon steam rising into the dim light. I ladled the gløgg into two ceramic mugs. Raisins. Sliced almonds. And finally, the finishing touch—a small plate of pepperkake, heart-shaped and fresh from the oven.

Her heart.

I had watched her smile at those before. I could not say when.

I knocked twice—habit, not necessity—and let myself into her suite. Silence greeted me, thick and close.

Cristabel lay curled on the sofa, not snoring—purring. A soft, steady hum in her throat. Her cheeks were flushed, her lips parted slightly, her hair fanned over the cushion in a way that twisted something deep and old inside me.

Beautiful in sleep.

I pressed my fingertips to my lips—an old blessing, older than language—remembering how easily they had found hers in the storm.

I reached for the woollen throw and covered her gently, tucking the edge beneath her arm so the draft from the window wouldn't touch her. My knuckles brushed her hip through the thin fabric of her dress.

I had forgotten restraint once before. I did not forget now.

The room smelled of birch sap and warm linen. Something else threaded through it—bright, unfamiliar, unmistakably hers.

I stepped back.

The house settled around her sleep, beams creaking softly. Outside, snow continued its patient work, reshaping the world one quiet layer at a time.

I stood alone in the corridor, hand resting against the wall, feeling the low thrum beneath the wood.

The house had waited.

I had pretended not to.

8

WHAT STAYED

Cristabel

Sleep weighs heavily, anchoring my limbs, while my thoughts drift into a place that isn't quite dreaming.

Grey skies split. Fire rises from the earth. A crystal vein glows beneath my feet—bright as diamonds, alive and humming. The air smells like iron and thawing earth.

The ground vibrates—not heat, but awareness.

It moves through bone instead of skin—not burning, but claiming.

The vein pulses once.

The flame touches my wrist where the vines live, tracing the ink as if it already knows the way.

"Who are you?" I whisper.

The flame answers—warm and certain.

It didn't frighten me. That was the strange part. It felt like contact, not threat. Like something answering when I hadn't known I'd called.

For a flicker, I'm not alone in it. There is another presence—

not inside the flame, not separate from it—but adjacent. Watching. Waiting.

I don't see him.

I feel him.

When I wake, my palms tingle. As if I'd touched something that hadn't let go.

"HEY, SLEEPYHEAD, WAKE UP!" Tiinná pounced onto the king-sized bed, straddling me in a tabletop pose. "Don't scream, okay. It's me, your maid of dishonour. Oh wow, look at you. You have no idea how much I've missed your face."

"Tiinná?" I sneaked a peek through sleep-heavy lashes and saw my best friend. She hadn't changed a bit. The same white gold hair hung past her shoulders. Her smile was just as bright. "How'd you get in here?"

"Stole the key." Tiinná puckered her shiny red lips and dangled a set of master keys from her long, delicate fingers. Dropping the keys, she wrapped her arms around me, the cold scent of winter's frost clinging to her coat.

"I had the strangest dream," I murmured, yawning.

The last thing I remembered was falling onto the sofa and nestling into the plush decorator pillows.

I woke to darkness.

Blue floor lights traced a quiet path to the king-sized bed. I followed them and slid beneath the duvet, the cotton cool at first, then warm where it sealed around me. I lay there, listening for the other shoe to drop. It didn't. Still, my muscles refused to release, as if my body didn't believe safety could be this quiet. I'd learned not to trust comfort that arrived too fast.

For me, it never came first.

"You'll be fine, trust me. A heaping load of waffles, slabs of brunost, and you'll be good to go." Her grin was contagious, her tinkling laughter lighter than snow.

"Brunost? The brown cheese? I had that last night." Pulling the duvet with me, I sat up and rested my head on the upholstered headboard as I looked around the dimly lit room. The drapes were drawn, leaving the bedroom doused in a twilight glow.

"Yeah, the brown cheese. Never mind that. You're here. You're really here." Her gaze darted over me, tears welling in her eyes, searching, checking, memorizing.

I let her look because I needed someone else to believe I was real again. I'd learned how easily the body could disappear before the mind was ready. My eyes closed for a brief second as I turned those thoughts away.

"I told you I'd come." I looked at her and smiled. For real this time. It had taken me years to make this trip. Life had gotten in the way.

She lifted my hair off my shoulder, separating the dark chunk. "Holy shit, C. Look at your hair. Did you do this?"

"Grew back that way. Snowy white with a devil's streak." I swept my hand through my hair, tossing my unique tresses to the side.

She stopped short when the duvet slipped off my shoulder, and the vines peeked out—dark ink threading from my wrist upward, curling over skin that once held stitches and surgical tape.

"Cris, is that?" Her voice weakened, her hand lifted, then paused, trembling just above my skin. "May I…?"

She waited for my answer like it mattered.

"Yes." I gazed into her crystal blue eyes. She had shared my pain with me long-distance. Only a phone call away, a quick text, a smiley emoji.

Her fingertip followed the line from wrist to rib, tracing the path the artist built to cover what the surgeons took.

One day, I was fine. The next, I wasn't. I swallowed the poisons. I underwent the surgeries. Slept. Puked. Slept again. The hospital sheets had that industrial starch smell that never left your skin. I learned the sound of IV pumps in my sleep.

And I kept on living.

Living wasn't bravery. It was stubbornness. Survival had trained me to accept intensity without panic.

"They're beautiful," she breathed. "Stronger than the scars, somehow."

"They've helped, you know? When I couldn't face myself or needed something that felt…alive." I traced my fingers over the vines inked into my skin. The days I spent in the tattoo studio were how I reminded myself I was still alive. Pain I chose felt different.

The ink began at my wrist—where the surgeons first marked me—and climbed upward in deliberate lines. The artist followed the map my body had already drawn, turning damage into something that moved.

I hadn't meant for it to feel like armour.

But sometimes armour chooses you.

"You're stronger than anyone I've ever known. You know that, right?" Tiinná blinked, swiping at her cheek.

"Some days." I tried for a smile, but my throat burned. I swallowed it down. Not today.

"I needed to see you before the wedding chaos tomorrow. I had to see with my own eyes that—that you made it." Her voice broke, and she scrubbed at her face.

"You know I did. You called me every day, remember?" I squeezed her hands. She was always emotional, but this was way over the top.

Outside, a gust of wind rattled the windowpane.

The vines tingled beneath my skin—soft. Like a pulse answering something outside the room. Not with heat. With awareness. The sensation followed a pattern—wrist to rib, rib to hip—the same route the flame traced in my dream.

It hadn't done that before Norway.

Tiinná didn't notice.

"Don't you ever scare me like that again." She pulled me into another fierce hug.

I had been scared. Part of me still was. Part of me always would be. I let her believe I hadn't.

I wanted to promise her. I didn't know if I could.

"Okay. Well. This is awesome, just freaking awesome. You've always been gorgeous, but now—now you look like a movie star. Drop the sheets, babe. Show me what you've got." She shifted into a cross-legged position beside me.

"Show you what?" I yawned, rubbed my eyes and yawned again.

"You know what. Those big, beautiful puppies," Tiinná yawned with me, then grinned. "Okay, stop that."

"All right. But only because I love you." I dropped the duvet, revealing my reconstructed breasts—new curves, unfamiliar weight, wholly mine. They weren't what I had before. They were what I had fought for.

"Yeah, right, C. You're the most out-there person I know. She traced her index finger over my prominent ribcage. Now this…this is stunning. I love how the vine wraps around your waist, and the roses crawl over your breasts. The dragonflies are beautiful." She tilted her head as she continued to inspect the vibrant tattoo.

I rolled my shoulders back, letting her inspect the work.

"The artist did a great job. You can't even see the scars. I want these." She ran her fingertips over each one. "How are you feeling? Good?"

"Yeah. Pretty much. Off to the races, so they say. Some days I don't even think about it." Rubbing the sleep from my eyes, I yawned again. "What time is it?"

The drapes parted, and in a flash of orange fur, Odin darted across the room, jumped onto the bed, and curled up between Tiinná and me. His purr grew louder as he nudged his head against my chin.

"What the hell? That cat doesn't like anybody, except Rurik." Her shoulders stiffened, and she sat back.

His name landed heavier than it should, as if it carried history. Heat ghosted across my lips for no reason I cared to examine.

I didn't try to explain that to myself. Explaining things was how I used to make them smaller.

Odin merely chirped. His single blue eye fixed on me—unblinking. It wasn't affectionate. It felt like judgment.

Outside, the wind shifted.

No—not the wind.

My skin prickled.

As if something had come nearer.

9

WAFFLES & WHISPERS

Cristabel

"And yet here he is, living his best life." I scratched behind Odin's ears, then lifted him into my arms, kissing the top of his head. "Fucking hell, Tiinná. You could have warned me."

"Warned you? About what?" Her brows creased, genuinely puzzled.

"Rurik? The innkeeper? I met him at the airport. Does he ever swear? Doesn't matter. I kissed him." Shivers ran through me—his warm lips, his deep laugh replaying without permission.

"You kissed Rurik?" Her voice dropped. Her eyes widened. "Oh my God. Spill the tea, girl."

"Yes. And he kissed me back." The memory came in pieces—pressure, warmth, the certainty of being held while the world moved. My throat caught. I remembered. Something. Why did he seem so familiar? Familiar didn't always mean known. Sometimes it meant something I hadn't finished.

"We stopped at a diner. For what do you call the late meal? The fourth dinner—kveldsmat, I think?" I placed my hand on my forehead, unable to hide my confusion. The night blurred in my mind.

"He took you for *kveldsmat*?" Her eyebrows lifted. She blinked and then grinned. "Of course he did."

I wasn't afraid of what it meant. I was afraid of how easily it fit.

I met her questioning gaze with mine, a flicker of fear running up my spine. With Tiinná, nothing was ever off the table.

"Norwegian men don't take a woman for real food, Cris. Not until the third or fourth date. It's a thing." She shook her head back and forth.

"The roads were bad. We had to stop." I studied my friend's quirky smile, replaying those moments. The snow. The wind. The glow in Rurik's eyes.

"Rurik won't mind the snow. He never has." Her lips curled into a subtle smile, revealing nothing. She said it casually, but her eyes didn't flicker.

That steadiness felt practiced. The way she said it told me this wasn't new information—just newly relevant.

"He said I look like a troll." I pulled the duvet up to my chin, displacing Odin. He settled, digging his claws into the fluffy duvet and positioning himself at the foot of the bed.

"A troll?" Ignoring the feral beast, she leaned in, twisting my hair into a topknot. "Ha, you kinda do, and I mean that in the most loving way. It's your hair, C—there's so much of it. Maybe it's your pointy nose and abnormally big ears." She pressed her lips together, squashing a giggle.

"He said if he makes me laugh, I have to marry him." The words landed and stayed. Familiar. Not heavy—just known. Like something I'd agreed to once and forgotten. I laughed because it felt safer than asking why the words stayed with me.

"That's Rurik. Always about the fairy tale. Now, let's go, girl. We're in a hurry." She bounced off the bed and crossed the room.

"Why do we have to hurry? What's the rush?" My radar piqued, telling me she was up to no good.

"Spa day with the boys. Pre-wedding tradition," she said lightly. "You'll see."

She pulled back the drapes, flooding the room with bright light. "Oh, look. Cookies."

"What spa day? And what boys?" I swung my feet onto the floor, anticipating her answer.

"Mine and yours. What could be more perfect? You and Rurik are practically an item. You have no idea what that means here," she added, almost under her breath. She sat in the armchair, a plate of cookies on her lap, crunching one after another.

"What does that mean?"

"Nothing." She grabbed another cookie too quickly. "It just means you won't be invisible."

"We're not an item. Jesus Christ… maybe we are." I lifted my hand, scratching the back of my head as the realization hit me. I kissed him, and I promised him a lot more. I think.

"So, what? Do you like him?" She offered me the plate. "Try one, they're amazing."

"Well. He's taking me to your wedding, if that's what

you want to know." I swallowed my morning breath, feeling more troll-like than ever.

"I am impressed, C. I have to say. You've gone from zero to sixty in no time at all. What's wrong? I know that look." She shifted sideways, unable to sit still.

"He doesn't know anything about me. About these." I gestured toward my chest as warmth gathered beneath my skin—slow, sure. Fear felt sharp. This didn't. Whatever this was, it wasn't fear asking me to hide. Or was it fear? No, I refused it. Fuck fear. I was done giving it oxygen.

"He's a teddy bear. And trust me—he's not lacking in confidence. You have nothing to worry about, C." Tiinná spread her hands wide. "There, okay? I've warned you."

What I wasn't saying was that confidence wasn't what drew me. The attraction went deeper than that.

"How do you know that?" A smile quirked on my face, my imagination taking flight.

"I'm his doctor." She held my gaze. "I'm everyone's doctor. Occupational hazard." She reached for another cookie without meeting my eyes. "When was the last time you got laid?"

"Um, Jack… it was with Jack." I squeezed my eyes shut, recalling a faded memory of a long-ago distant time.

"Jack? That Jack? You're not wasting time with him, are you?" She dropped her chin, her piercing gaze filled with attitude.

"No, we broke up, remember?" I let the old out and the new in. That's what they say. That's what they say. I didn't tell her at the first sign of trouble, he took off like a scared jackrabbit.

"And I remember that was a very long two years ago.

You haven't had sex since?" She stood and rested her hands on her hips, her eyes running over me.

"I just… haven't wanted to." Wanting had felt like a luxury for a long time. I smiled, knowing Tiinná would run a marathon with that one.

"Jesus, C., I've left you alone for far too long. Look, sweet pea, it's time you got on with your life, and I'm making sure that happens. Have a shower, okay? You stink." She waved her hand back and forth, scrunching her nose.

"You think so?" I stuck my nose into my armpit, inhaling the scent of buttercups and black beans. Not a good smell.

"I love you, girlfriend. But, yes. We need to clean you up and get you laid—this weekend." She clapped her hands together and walked away, leaving me alone in the bedroom.

"This weekend?" I rolled that idea over and over and over. Somehow, I was okay with Tiinná's plan.

For the first time in years, the future didn't feel like something to endure.

The Tiinná I loved, with her arms raised, did a happy dance.

I observed her as she had observed me. Tall and willowy, she could be a runway model. The way her eyes glinted. "Did you get contacts?"

"What? No." She pulled a red hat over her head and then looked into the floor mirror, tilting her face back and forth as she admired her reflection.

"Oh—I just… never mind." I waved it off and smiled, even though something tightened low in my chest. She was right. I was in Norway. I was alive. That should've been enough. I told myself that wanting more didn't mean something was wrong with me.

I wandered to the window, tugged the curtain aside. Everything looked like a Christmas card—snow-piled roofs, wood smoke drifting into a blue morning sky.

Still, something tugged at the back of my mind—shadows where there shouldn't be any. I knew the difference between instinct and imagination.

I pushed it aside. If it needed a name, it would ask for one.

"Wow," I breathed. "This place is… unreal."

"It's fucking freezing, C. Deep freeze all this week. "Oh, and tonight? Engagement party at the pub. Everyone will be there." She said it lightly—but her eyes held mine.

"Everyone?" I repeated.

"Røros isn't big. When something matters, people show up. "They've been waiting."

"For what?"

She smiled. "You. Now, hurry. I'm taking you out for breakfast."

The word *everyone* settled differently than it should have.

Movement felt safer than stillness.

Tonight I would meet his world.

Not the version of him that leaned in slowly and let me decide.

The version everyone else already knew.

10

WINTER HAS A MEMORY

C*ristabel*

I pulled a sweater over my head and slipped into my jeans. She barely gave me time to brush my teeth before dragging me into the hallway, her long strides reaching the entrance door in no time.

"Wait, I don't remember where my coat is." I pulled my hair into a braid and tucked the length under my sweater.

Her eyebrows arched as she pointed to the hotel's foyer and a row of coats hanging in an open closet.

"Okay. Okay." I grabbed my coat and pulled my boots on one at a time.

From nearby, dishes clattered. I turned around and caught sight of a grand reception room with a blazing fire-place, bookshelves, comfy chairs, and sofas. Couples sitting together, coffee mugs in hand. An elderly man read a newspaper. A child sprawled on the carpet with a puzzle. Rurik was nowhere in sight.

I noticed his absence more than I should and didn't like that either. Not missing. Just aware.

"Where are we headed?" I followed her out the door of Rurik's hotel and into the courtyard—straight into a wall of freezing air.

The cold slapped my face, needling my cheeks, slicing through even my thickest sweater as if it knew every soft place to strike.

Pain sharpened my focus. That, at least, was familiar. The cold found the gap at my wrists where my gloves didn't quite meet my sleeves. The skin there felt thinner now. Awake.

My breath fogged, drifting upward like a ghost fleeing my mouth.

"This way." She power-walked away from the hotel and onto the snow-covered street. "You'll fall madly in love—you'll call quits to the wet and windy Toronto scene, and you'll live happily ever after here in Røros."

She didn't look at me when she said it. She looked ahead. Like she was describing something already underway.

I didn't answer because imagining it felt dangerous in a way I couldn't yet describe.

"What? Whoa, Tiinná, slow down." I stuffed my hands into my pockets, my boots skating over the icy snow.

"There's an opening in Røros for a veterinarian." She met my eyes. "I mentioned you."

I stopped walking.

"You what?"

"Just in case." She held my stare a beat too long. "Old Lars Jensson ran off to somewhere warm with someone younger. Details are fuzzy. You can start with my mom's reindeer herd. Their vaccinations are overdue." Her excitement was evident in the rise and fall of her voice.

"Your mom's reindeer? You want me to check on a herd of reindeer?" My frozen breath hung in the air. My heart stopped—then kicked back to life with a frantic thump. Stay in Røros with Tiinná? Relocate my entire life to the Arctic Circle? I chewed on that.

Big ideas had a way of sounding reasonable when you were far from home.

"Yes, the whole herd. Don't worry. Reindeer are just like big cows. I told you, C., I've got this." She looped her arm through mine, holding me upright.

"This place feels like a storybook." Not make-believe. Preserved. I gazed at the old smithy and the open-air workshop, just as a man stepped out, tall, blond, striking. His shadow stretched behind him, but the light was in front of him. I stared after him. "Did you see him?"

A pulse sparked at my wrist—small, precise—then threaded inward, tracing the ink.

"Hmm?" She popped a lingonberry candy into her mouth. "See what?"

Her eyes flicked—not to where I was looking, but slightly above it, like she'd measured the same thing and chosen not to name it.

I watched him disappear around the corner, taking his shadow with him. I trusted my eyes. I just didn't trust the conclusion yet.

People moved around us—locals heading to work, tourists pointing excitedly at shop windows—but a few of them cast quick glances my way.

I'd learned what it felt like to be watched for weakness. This wasn't that.

Then the cobblestones beneath my boots gave a soft thrum—slow. Patient.

My breath hitched. I waited for fear to arrive. It didn't. I told myself it was the cold. I swallowed hard and hurried to catch up with her.

"Listen. If you go out at night, don't take the alleys." She motioned toward the shadowy alleyways, some with names, shortcuts to unknown places.

"Why?" I wondered where they led, not that I had any intention of wandering the back alleys of a strange town late at night. Even this pretty little place had secrets.

"This is an old mining town. The tunnels make people uneasy. Best not to test them." The kind of advice meant to keep something sleeping.

My mouth hung open. She shrugged.

"Shift?" I looked at my feet, at the snow-packed ground.

"Old miner's stories. Echoes. Whispers. One guy swore he saw a shadow running along the ceiling." Her eyes looked worried. She paused. "Just stories."

The correction felt practiced.

"Tiinná." I crossed my arms over my chest.

"It's just stories. Here we are." She walked ahead, up the six steps to a bakery.

I didn't laugh it off, either. Some warnings weren't meant to scare—just to narrow your choices. I chose not to panic. Panic had never helped me listen. Stillness did.

"Cris?"

I looked up as the bell chimed, and Tiinná breezed inside, the cold air swirling after her. I didn't walk. I ran up the steps.

Sweet heat enveloped me—spice, sugar, and the rich buttery aroma of something heavenly.

Conversations didn't stop—but they thinned. Not silence, an adjustment in tone.

A woman at the counter held my gaze a second too long before nodding once—not polite. Intentional.

Tiinná didn't react—but her posture eased. Like something had checked a box.

"Do I have something on my face?" I murmured.

Tiinná didn't look at me. "No."

She was already at the counter before I could even read the chalkboard menu, grinning like she knew every secret in the room.

"Two chai lattes," she told the barista, then angled her head toward me. "And one *vaffel* for my guest. Extra partridgeberry jam."

"How do you even know I want that?" I gazed at the cast-iron griddle, my mouth watering.

"You always liked waffles. Don't pretend. You used to steal mine all the time." She handed me a tray.

"That was a long time ago." I laughed, stunned she would remember such a trivial thing.

"Enough for you to forget, but not enough for me to stop ordering for you." Her smile calmed my racing heart.

The barista slid the order slip across the counter.

Tiinná snatched it up, humming a tune I didn't recognize, something soft and strange. Irish maybe?

I shook my head. She knew me too well. Almost… eerily well.

I gazed at the people, listening to the mingling of voices speaking unfamiliar languages, at the muted shades of green and wooden tables with yellow-painted chairs.

At the counter, the baker lifted a waffle from the iron—five delicate hearts joined in a circle, edges lacy and crisp, the centre pale and soft. He spooned the jam over it—ruby-red, glossy, unmistakable.

A shimmer passed under the plate, like light bending where it shouldn't. When I blinked, it was gone. I marked it as real without deciding what it meant.

"Sit. You need something hot." Her smile tightened. She linked arms as we moved toward a corner table. "Sugar. Caffeine. Preferably all at once. So, did you sleep well?"

"Odin slept across my neck. I woke up half-asphyxiated and covered in cat hair." I tried—and failed—to sound casual. Odin had refused to leave the hotel room. He sat there, blinking from the bed as if he could protect me better from that spot. *Treasonous little fur god.* I already missed him.

"That cat is crazy." She slid into the seat across from me with a smug grin.

I also had strange dreams—waterfalls, runes I didn't recognize, the sensation of someone holding my hand in another time—but I wasn't about to mention that. Some things felt private even from my best friend.

I sank back into the chair, my throat tight, the waffle waiting on its plate. I took a forkful.

It melted on my tongue, the red berries bursting, tart and wild with a sweetness like winter sun hitting fresh snow.

Then—a pulse. Low. Deep. From the vines beneath my sweater. Like the diner. Like his hand.

My body reacted before my thoughts did. That didn't make it wrong.

"God, this is good." I swallowed hard, trying to steady my voice.

Tiinná's gaze dropped to my wrist. Not to the fork. To where the ink began. She stared too long, then smiled.

"What's going on, Tiinná. Why do I feel like I belong here?"

"Some places feel familiar." She stirred her latte slowly.

"Especially when they've been waiting for the right time."

I didn't argue. I just didn't surrender to it either. "Tiinná…what does this place think it knows about me?"

"Some places know who fits." Her eyes lifted to mine. "And this one… Makes room. You don't stand out here, C. You settle."

Her words left a strange flavour in my mouth. I shifted my feet, crossing them beneath the table.

I glanced down at my hands, half-expecting to see them outlined against the tabletop, like a paper cutout someone had already traced. The pulse under my skin hadn't faded. If anything, it held.

Outside the window, snow slid from a roof in a single clean sheet, vanishing without a sound.

I didn't like how right it felt. Right had fooled me before.

The vines pulsed once—not warning. Confirmation. This time it didn't climb. It held. As if something had arrived.

I pressed my palms flat to the table, grounding myself in wood and coffee.

"Okay. That's new."

Tiinná didn't flinch.

"It's not."

11

THE MOMENT THAT ARRIVED

C*ristabel*

"So, tell me everything." Her eyes twinkled.

My body loosened for the first time since the flight. I stabbed another piece of waffle. "You know everything. There's nothing more to tell."

"Hmm," Tiinná hummed. "Just you meeting the hottest man in Scandinavia at the airport, kissing him, arranging a fuck date, and him personally driving you to his hotel and installing you in his suite of rooms. Nothing at all."

"My room… " I looked up from the decadent pastry. "Not his room."

"Did I say that?" She blinked. "Huh."

"You're acting weird." My eyes narrowed.

"You bring it out in me."

She'd always been like that.

I smiled at her, the old reflex kicking in, the one that said *she's dramatic but harmless, this is just Tiinná being Tiinná*.

But the smile didn't quite settle. It froze on my face, then slipped.

I'd known Tiinná long enough to recognize that look—the one she got when she thought something was already in motion and was waiting to see who else would notice.

She stirred her latte even though the foam had already settled, the spoon circling once, twice, three times.

The café noise shifted, then returned.

The spoon in Tiinná's cup clinked once, sharp and loud, then stopped.

Someone called out an order—*oat latte for—*

The name never came.

My stomach dipped, like an elevator stopping a floor too soon. I shifted on the chair, the wooden seat cold even through my jeans.

My knee pressed harder into the underside of the table, the solid edge grounding me. I checked my phone without meaning to. No new messages. No missed calls. The time hadn't changed.

The café rushed back into itself, sound flooding the space like water finding a crack. Laughter, dishes, the hiss of milk foam. Normal again.

"You're deflecting." I exhaled, annoyed that I'd noticed—and more annoyed that it mattered.

She didn't deny it.

I half-listened, my attention drawn to the man at a nearby table. His laughter cut through the room—too sharp, too bright. When he smiled, his teeth caught the light oddly, longer than I expected. I blinked, and the moment slid back into place, ordinary again.

He looked at me then.

Not openly—just long enough to register. Just a fraction too long, like someone checking a reflection in glass. His smile never changed, but his eyes sharpened.

I shifted, angling my body away from him. Tiinná didn't follow my gaze. No one did. The man laughed again, perfectly normal. Perfectly human. Which didn't undo what I'd noticed. I trusted that reaction more than the explanation I didn't have yet. Still, I didn't turn back.

"Spa day with the boys. And Rurik's already in." Her grin caught me off guard.

"Excuse me? What?" I turned and faced my friend.

"Hot pool. Cold pool. Sauna. Must've slipped my mind." She nodded—convincing me not at all.

"I don't have a bathing suit." A spike of doubt hit hard and fast, out of proportion to the moment. Why this sudden trepidation? Why now?

The café closed in all at once, the air pressing against my skin. I rolled my shoulders, trying to shake it off, annoyed with myself for reacting to nothing at all.

"No bathing suits in Norway, C. Au naturel." She flashed me another grin, the devil dancing in her eyes.

Heat climbed my neck, unwelcome and sudden.

It wasn't modesty—at least, not exactly. I'd never been precious about bodies. But the idea landed wrong. Steam. Skin. Exposure. Not nakedness—attention.

I laughed it off because that's what I did when things made me uncomfortable. Humour first. Questions later. It had gotten me through worse. Still, something stayed with me. Not the words—the pause beneath them.

A pressure, low and steady, like my body had leaned forward without telling me why. As if something had been waiting for it.

My fingers worried at my napkin, folding and unfolding the edge until the paper softened.

Why this tightness in my chest over something so stupid? I shoved the feeling aside and reached for my fork.

"Naked?" I examined my stubby fingernail.

"What are you worried about? You're beautiful. Everything about you is beautiful. Even your skinny ass, come on, C. Rurik's got a hard-on for you. And Lars has eyes only for me. What's the big deal? You've basically scheduled a fuck-date with him. The couples massage will be a piece of cake."

"I did not… He asked me to your…" I stopped mid-sentence. I could not deny my attraction to Handsome Man.

"So, there you go. The spa will be a piece of cake, and the couple's massage." She winked at me.

Of course she did.

"Couple's massage? What? No." I gasped. Damn her. Had I never won a discussion with Tiinná? Like never.

"Soft music. Essential oils. That happily ever after moment." She winked again, emphasizing her point.

I remembered Rurik's big hands and long fingers. The thought landed low and slow, settling in a place that had been quiet for far too long. I stilled, because moving only made it worse. How skilled might his hands be? Jack thought he was stuffing a turkey for Thanksgiving dinner.

"Where's your sense of adventure, C? Maybe you'll even enjoy an orgasm or two or three?"

"Shit fuck, Tiinná." I chewed my bottom lip.

Written in the stars?

"Aren't you already having sexy dreams about the man? A little coo-coo-ca-choo? It's what you need. Don't deny it." She said it lightly, but her eyes stayed on me a fraction too long—not probing, not suspicious. Just watching. Her blue eyes held steady.

I opened my mouth to argue—and froze.

Something tightened at my wrist. Not pain. Not heat. A precise pull — as if the ink had drawn breath. It didn't travel this time. It held.

My fork hovered midair.

I lowered it slowly, annoyed now, more than anything. Annoyed at my body. At Tiinná. At this town that smelled like bread and snow and secrets I hadn't asked for.

Something pooled low beneath my ribs. I pressed my palm flat to my stomach, embarrassed by the instinct, as if that might quiet it.

For no reason I could name, I knew someone was coming. Not because I'd been waiting—because something else had.

Tiinná stopped talking. She didn't look surprised. She looked ready.

I didn't look at the door. I didn't need to.

My shoulders straightened on their own.

The air shifted—subtle, wrong, unmistakable.

I drew in a slow breath and held it.

The bell above the café door rang.

12

THE STRANGER WHO WASN'T

C*ristabel*

The bell over the bakery door chimed. My breath caught, the sound landing low in my chest—not sharp, not startling. Just there.

I didn't turn right away. I didn't need to.

Across the room, a chair scraped. Someone laughed and then went quiet.

Ridiculous. Doors opened all the time. People came and went. This was a bakery, not a prophecy.

Still, my hand tightened around the fork, my pulse ticking just behind my jaw.

I took one more breath before looking up. It occurred to me that I hadn't finished my coffee. The waffle was cooling. There were a hundred small, ordinary things I could still choose instead.

I didn't choose them.

When I finally looked up, it didn't feel like surprise. It felt like something arriving exactly where it meant to.

Rurik stepped inside, snow dusting his shoulders and

melting into dark drops down the leather, his hair damp at the ends, as if he'd come from the woods or somewhere insanely cold. The moment his eyes met mine, the pulse at my wrist snapped once.

"Right on schedule."

My heart kicked. "How did he… "

She only lifted an eyebrow. "Small town." Then, softer, "Whatever you think you know about Rurik… just remember you don't owe him anything." Her tone stayed casual. Her eyes didn't leave me.

I searched her face for the joke, the punchline, but found none. Just that same watchfulness she'd had all morning.

"You're being weird."

Her mouth curved. "I'm being careful."

Careful had edges.

The café suddenly felt thinner—windows fogged but fragile, sound carrying too easily. Tiinná didn't do careful. She did bold and loud and certain. This was different.

I wondered, not for the first time that morning, how long she'd been watching me.

The ink at my wrist tightened once beneath my sleeve.

I dropped my gaze to the table, suddenly aware of how much I didn't know—about this place, about her, about the man walking toward us like he belonged there.

"What's underneath?" I blinked, pulse fluttering. The question escaped before I could decide who it was for.

Tiinná's smile sharpened—too knowing, too amused to be comforting. "Ask him. If he trusts you, maybe he'll even tell you." She nudged me with her elbow. "And stop looking at him like that, or he's going to melt into a puddle."

My gaze jerked back to my waffle like it was suddenly the most fascinating thing in Norway. But when Rurik crossed the room, his every step measured and unhurried, the vines hummed against my skin. Alive.

He didn't scan the room. Didn't hesitate. He moved like the space between us had already been cleared.

People shifted—chairs angling, shoulders turning just enough to clear a path. Conversations dipped, then resumed.

I noticed the way the light caught on his shoulders, the slow drip of melting snow darkening the leather, the steadiness of his hands at his sides.

My chest tightened, and then something clicked into place. As if I'd been standing slightly off-center and hadn't known it.

"Cristabel." He paused at our table, his eyes fixed on me like I were the only person in the room.

The name carried farther than it should have. Sound travelled differently around him. A few heads turned. Not openly—just enough to register the sound before returning to their conversations.

No one was speaking very loudly anymore.

I'd forgotten how he said my name—slow, careful, like it mattered.

"You fell asleep before I could say goodnight. I came to make sure you were all right." His voice—a soothing caress.

"Tiinná wanted waffles." My pulse jumped. My reaction to this man didn't make sense.

"I *always* want waffles." Tiinná lifted her latte with a serene smile.

Rurik ignored Tiinná entirely. His gaze lowered to my plate, softening slightly. "You like lingonberries?"

I nodded, confused and a little breathless. "It's tart. Comforting. I don't know, it just feels right."

Rurik exhaled slowly—almost in relief. "It would." The words landed like confirmation, not opinion.

I waited for him to explain. People usually did when they said things like that—backpedalled, joked, corrected course.

He didn't.

The silence that followed wasn't awkward. It was full. Dense enough that I could feel it pressing at the base of my throat.

"Did Odin stay with you?"

"He did. He stole half the bed." I nodded.

That softened his whole expression. "He only does that when he feels someone needs company."

As if the cat were a better judge than most people.

My heart stuttered.

Tiinná made a violent coughing sound. "Well, I should, uh—check on the—napkins."

"There are napkins right here." I sent her a furtive glance.

"Yes, but those might not be folded enough." Tiinná pointed vaguely.

I watched her vanish toward the counter. "She's acting deranged."

Rurik's lips twitched. "She's fond of you."

"But why does she keep—"

He leaned closer, his voice dropping into something that made the vines along my ribs answering. "I didn't want last night to be the only time I saw you."

"You invited me to Tiinná's wedding," I whispered back. "And apparently you're spending your day at the spa with a stranger."

"You don't feel like a stranger." His gaze softened—too soft for someone I'd just met.

The words landed with more weight than he could have known. I'd expected that sentence to feel flattering. Or flirtatious. Or reckless enough that I could laugh it off.

The words didn't flirt. They landed like something resumed.

Heat pooled in my cheeks. I didn't know what to do with that.

I searched his face for irony, for flirtation, for the easy charm I could deflect with a joke. There was none. Just quiet certainty—and something else, held carefully behind it, as if he were choosing restraint over instinct.

My skin warmed again, the vines responding with a low, steady pulse.

I swallowed. "You say that like it means something."

"Okay! Spa day!" Behind Rurik, Tiinná clapped her hands sharply, pointing vaguely between them. "Mountain. Hot pools. See you later, Andersen."

"Right now? Why?" I blinked.

Tiinná winked. "Because destiny is prettier with steam and mountain views."

I stared at both of them. Totally confused. But the vines answered again—low and steady.

So when Rurik held out his hand, I didn't hesitate.

My body was already moving.

Rurik

Cristabel laughed at something Tiinná tossed across the table, bright and unguarded. The sound carried.

I watched the ripple move outward—not visible, not dramatic, but real all the same. A man near the window lowered his paper without realizing he'd stopped reading. The woman by the hearth paused mid-sip. Even the baker hesitated before turning his waffle iron.

Most of them wore their humanity well. They always had. The mountain attracted the old and the patient, sheltering things that preferred not to be named. Barrow-keepers with borrowed faces. Forest-born spirits who learned to sit at tables. Land-wights bound to beam and stone. None of them was the threat. They were only reacting to what brushed against them.

Cristabel shifted toward the door, and her sleeve slipped back just enough to reveal the first curl of ink at her wrist. The air altered—not dramatically, not in a way anyone else would register, but enough. A faint tightening moved through the room, subtle as breath drawn through snow.

There it was.

The binding did not flare. It tightened—measured, restrained. It was never forged for laughter. It was wrought in darker hours, when blood answered blood and a heart was sealed beneath rock that remembers every name spoken above it. My line did not inherit a legend. We inherited a lock.

And locks remember what they hold.

Across the room, Tiinná's gaze lifted—not to Cristabel's face, but to her wrist. Only for a second. Long enough.

When her eyes met mine, she did not smile. The smallest shake of her head.

Not here.

Cristabel pushed open the door, and the bell chimed, bright and domestic, absurdly ordinary against the tension beneath it. Snowlight spilled in around her, silver and clean. She did not feel the faint strain threading through the stone below Røros—the quiet resistance of something testing its reach.

The others would circle. They would watch. They would measure her brightness the way old things measure heat in winter. That, I could manage. I had managed it before.

What lay deeper was different.

If it rose without restraint, it would not ask who she was. It would decide.

Tiinná followed her into the street, still talking about steam caves and hot pools, laughter trailing behind her as if nothing in this town had teeth. But as she passed, her fingers brushed the doorframe—a small, deliberate touch against old wood. Acknowledgment. Warning.

Perhaps both.

I remained where I was a moment longer, listening the way my father taught me—through the soles of my feet, through bone, through the silence beneath sound. The mountain had turned.

Not awakening.

But aware.

I moved for the door.

Not because Cristabel was fragile.

Some debts wake the moment they sense the hand that sealed them.

I would not let her stand alone when they wake.

13

GIRL TALK

C*ristabel*

The bakery door shut behind us, the bell chiming bright.

Cold air hit my cheeks and cleared the sugar from my lungs. I drew it in. It was the kind of breath that stings on the way down.

The street looked staged for a postcard—timbered storefronts, garlands pinned over doorframes, wooden stalls unwrapped for the Christmas market.

A man untangled a string of lights, swearing under his breath. Another dragged a crate of oranges over cobblestones, boots slipping. He glanced at Tiinná and gave a short nod. She lifted her chin back like she'd known him since childhood.

Someone tested a speaker; a burst of tinny carol skipped into the air before cutting out.

The whole place was already moving.

Tiinná slipped her arm through mine and steered me

toward the curb. A woman across the street paused mid-sweep and watched us go by. Not curious—just taking note. "Hydrate before you fornicate." She bumped her shoulder into mine and waggled her brows.

I choked on a laugh, covering my mouth. "You are unbelievable," I murmured, heat creeping into my cheeks. I was grateful for the cold.

"I'm efficient." She tossed back her hair and stood a little taller.

Rurik walked on my other side—close. Not touching, but near enough that I felt him through my coat. When a delivery truck reversed too quickly behind us, his hand hovered briefly at the small of my back, protective without being possessive, never quite landing.

I noticed anyway.

We passed the skating rink in the centre square. A towering Christmas tree glittered even in daylight, ornaments flashing when the wind shifted.

Children sat on a wooden bench, tying skates with bared fingers while a boy attempted a dramatic spin and wiped out with a spectacular faceplant.

Laughter lifted into the cold, from the boy, from his friends. A woman called to him, her expression more exasperated than worried.

Beyond the square, the train pulled into the station in a bloom of steam, metal shrieking as it settled. Passengers stepped down wrapped in scarves and wool hats, boots crunching over packed snow.

A woman glided past us on a kick sled, groceries stacked neatly on the runner in front of her.

"This place isn't real," I slowed, turned in a slow circle, taking it all in.

"It's just Tuesday," Tiinná tugged me forward, before I froze solid.

In a storefront window, I caught our reflection—three figures in winter light. For half a second, I thought there was someone taller behind us.

I blinked.

Garlands. Pine boughs. My imagination.

Ginger cats lounged everywhere. One curled outside the cobbler's shop. Another perched beneath the butcher's window. A third sprawled across folded blankets at a wool stall, tail flicking lazily as if supervising the morning.

"Are all the gingers in Norway required to live here?" I tipped my chin toward one of them.

Tiinná glanced at the cat, then at Rurik. Her smile tilted slightly. "They keep things tidy." She brushed snow off my sleeve as she said it.

A curtain twitched in the window above the cobbler's shop. I couldn't tell if it was the draft or someone stepping back. The cat by the cobbler's door didn't blink when we passed. Its eyes tracked me, unhurried.

Rurik's jaw shifted just once before smoothing out.

A shutter moved somewhere above us. A door closed just a little too fast. Under the noise, a faint vibration through my boots.

I rubbed my palm over my ribs and kept walking.

"It's like walking inside a snow globe." I tucked my hair behind my ear, breath fogging between us.

His gaze moved once more over the rooflines, the narrow alleys, the dark seam of forest at the far end of town. For a brief second, his expression tightened. His attention shifted, like he'd heard something I hadn't.

"It grows on you." His gaze held mine.

"I already like it." I shrugged, shy under his gaze.

His mouth curved, small and knowing. "I know."

We reached Tiinná's car—a sleek black Audi polished to a mirror shine, indecently modern against the timbered buildings.

It was parked in front of the red wooden house she shared with three other girls from town—white trim, steep roof, boots lined up on the steps like sentries.

The car's interior smelled faintly of citrus and leather. Everything inside was immaculate, even the charging cable coiled neatly in its cradle.

"Spa," Tiinná declared. "Before the two of you combust in public."

"I am not combusting." I folded my arms, which made her grin wider.

Rurik leaned toward my open window. The air between us tightened.

"For balance."

"Balance of what?" I lifted my chin, daring him.

His gaze flicked briefly toward the treeline beyond town. Then lower. Toward the stone foundations beneath the buildings. Just for a heartbeat.

"Heat." His gaze slid back to mine.

Before I could press him, Tiinná eased the car into motion.

We rolled past a two-storey red house with a sharply pitched roof and white trim. Smoke curled from the chimney in a thin ribbon.

"Five minutes," Tiinná announced, already unbuckling. "Something borrowed."

She bounded up the steps and disappeared inside without knocking.

I stayed in the passenger seat, watching snowflakes fall. The street had gone quieter here. The market noise felt distant, muted by walls and wood and time.

A truck rolled past.

Dark. Familiar.

Rurik.

He didn't slow, but two fingers lifted from the steering wheel as he disappeared around the bend. As if he knew exactly where we were headed—and would arrive before us without needing directions.

I twisted in my seat to watch the taillights vanish around the bend.

For a moment, the ground beneath the car gave the faintest tremor. Not enough to shake anything loose—only a subtle shift beneath packed snow and old stone. Then nothing.

An orange cat sat on the neighbour's doorstep, tail wrapped neatly around its paws. Another crouched beneath a birch tree across the road.

They weren't thin or skittish. They just watched.

I looked away first.

Tiinná reappeared carrying a small linen-wrapped parcel and slid back into the driver's seat, breath puffing white.

"Got it."

The cats were gone.

We left the centre of town and the road curved almost immediately into forest—dense pine and birch rising on either side like cathedral columns. Snow softened the world into something hushed and bright. The tires hummed over packed white.

The trees stood too close to the road, branches reaching

toward the car as we passed, snow sliding off in soft thuds.

"You're quiet." She glanced at me without turning her head.

"Just taking it in." I traced a finger through the fog on the window.

"You're thinking about him." She smirked.

"I am not." I looked straight ahead.

"You are absolutely thinking about him." She laughed and turned the dial higher.

The trees thinned into a clearing brushed in silver, and I saw him before I fully understood what I was looking at —a stag standing just beyond the reach of the road, his body dark against the snow, antlers branching wide enough to hold the pale sky between their points.

Tiinná eased off the gas without speaking, and the car slowed in a way that felt less like a decision and more like instinct.

He wasn't grazing. He wasn't startled, either. Steam left his nostrils in slow, steady bursts that rose and dissolved into the cold, and there was something unnervingly composed in the way he held himself, as though he had chosen to stand there.

He looked directly at me.

Not at the windshield. Not at the shape of the car.

At me.

My pulse dropped. I leaned forward without realizing I'd moved, one hand braced against the dash, the heat from the vents brushing my knees while the rest of me went very still.

For a long moment, neither of us blinked.

Then he dipped his head—not sharply, not in alarm, but slowly as if acknowledging something I hadn't yet named.

Snow slid from a branch behind him, the soft thud breaking whatever had stretched between us, and my jaw tightened before I even knew it had. I swallowed and tasted metal at the back of my tongue.

He stepped backward once, then again, each movement unhurried, until the trunks swallowed him and the space he'd occupied looked empty again.

The engine hummed.

"They get bold this time of year." Tiinná's hands tightened briefly on the steering wheel.

"That wasn't bold." My voice came out rough. I cleared my throat. "That was… enormous."

A quick laugh from her, a little too sharp, and her foot pressed down on the gas.

I twisted in my seat and watched the clearing until it slipped behind us, and for a strange, fleeting second, I had the sense that if I stepped out into that snow and stood exactly where he had stood, something inside me would settle into place—or split open.

I rubbed my arms, cold shooting through me.

The spa appeared through the trees in a wash of glass and timber, steam rising into the cold air in pale ribbons. As we pulled into the lot, warmth flickered in my palms.

I flexed my fingers.

Tiinná parked and killed the engine.

"Ready to sweat?"

I looked once more at the treeline, at the snow resting untouched on stone and branch.

Everything appeared ordinary.

Still.

I opened the door.

"Let's find out."

A red squirrel chattered from an oak as we crossed the path. It darted from snow-dusted branches to the thatched roof of a log cutter's cabin. I searched the shadowy underbrush for the Big Bad Wolf.

A woman in a black sauna skirt and matching bandeau struck a copper gong once, then twice, calling guests to the sauna ritual.

Inside, the lobby smelled of cedar and citrus. A woman behind the reception desk looked up as we entered, her hair braided tight against her head.

"Velkommen," she greeted, already reaching beneath the counter.

Tiinná leaned in. "Two for the ritual."

The woman's gaze flicked briefly to me—measured, not unkind—before she handed over two folded robes and a stack of towels. "Changing rooms are through the glass corridor. Lockers on the left."

Her fingers brushed mine as she passed the robe. Warm. Dry. Steady.

I swallowed.

"You're going to love this. Aufguss is the hottest wellness trend." Tiinná glanced sideways, urging me onward.

"Aufguss?" I followed Tiinná, my feet flopping in loose-fitting spa slippers—the complimentary ones from the Norwegian Wellness Spa—while zen-like music gently guided each weary guest toward enlightenment—or heat stroke.

"Yes, it's evocative. Inspiring, even. Trust me, you

won't be bored." She brushed my shoulder and sailed past me into the sauna hall like she owned the place.

"Oh, I'm not bored." I stood on the heated stones, admiring the oval-shaped wooden door. The air felt thicker here. Quieter. Voices dropped when we stepped in. My naked body on display for the first time in how many years?

I braced for panic.

It never arrived.

"Come on, C, lose the robe." Tiinná held my gaze, her arms loose at her sides, breasts perky, stomach flat.

Tiinná stood easy in her skin. I envied that. I let the doubt pass through me.

She motioned toward a row of hooks.

"Okay. Okay." I dug in my robe pocket and layered my lips with a waxy film of lip chap.

"Stop it, C." Tiinná clapped her hands.

"Stop what?" I lifted a brow and hung my robe on the hook, wrapping the complimentary towel around myself. Overlapping the edges over the swell of my breasts, I faced her. She knew exactly what I was thinking.

"The towel is for sitting on." She reached for it, smiling that knowing, infuriating smile.

I glanced once at the hallway behind us—the hooks, the door, the way back still open.

"Okay. Okay, I got it." I kicked off my slippers, then scooped them up and tucked them into my robe sleeve before following Tiinná into the heat.

Wet, eucalyptus-laced air pressed against my skin, making my eyes water and my lungs sting. The room breathed—slow inhales of steam, slow exhalations of heat. I gazed at benches filled with people, all naked or nearly so, settling on neatly folded towels, skin shining with sweat.

"Hello, boys," Tiinná announced our presence.

She'd been right about Lars earlier: pudgy cheeks, watery eyes, steam-fogged steel-framed glasses. Adorable in his own way.

Black spots danced before my eyes as I took a deep, steadying breath, my heart pounding to an erratic beat. Men and women from all walks of life lounged, chatting easily, completely comfortable in their own skin. I focused on the rows of feet and followed the right pair upward.

Rurik—bare, heat-sheened, seated in the front row. His eyes lifted when I entered.

Everyone here was naked. That wasn't the problem.

It was the way his attention settled on me—quiet, unmistakable.

The noise dulled.

I gripped the towel in front of my chest like a shield. Not because of him. Because I was very aware of myself, of being seen without having decided how much I wanted to reveal.

Tiinná leaned close. "Remember, towel goes under your butt, not around you."

"Do people really do this here?" I whispered, my throat closing.

"It's Norway, sweetheart. Shame is optional. Hydration is mandatory." She grinned, her eyes dancing with light.

I wanted to evaporate.

"Oh, good—he saved us seats. Bench twelve." She elbowed me.

"He—what?" My heart seized.

Tiinná didn't answer. She grabbed Lars's wrist and started climbing toward the top row.

"Tiinná, wait." I swallowed hard.

"Better heat up here! Enjoy!" Then she and Lars vanished into the upper benches, leaving me standing in the aisle.

She would.

14

HEAT THAT WAKES THE BONES

C*ristabel*

A flicker of heat moved through me—not anger exactly, but something sharp enough to sting. This wasn't accidental. Tiinná had orchestrated this with the precision of someone who knew exactly which buttons to press.

Naked, panicking, and standing directly in front of Rurik like an offering I hadn't agreed to be.

"Round one starts momentarily. Please sit." The Aufgussmeister clapped his hands sharply.

My body locked before my mind caught up.

Rurik rose from the bench, unhurried. The movement drew a few nearby glances before anyone realized they'd looked. Steam slid down his shoulders in thin white ribbons, curling and breaking as he moved. He didn't close the distance. He didn't need to. The room adjusted for him. He looked at me—and the air between us drew taut, as if something had taken hold of it.

He was beautiful in a way that felt intentional, entirely at ease in his skin while mine threatened to betray me.

My fingers clenched the towel tighter, knuckles white.

"Cristabel." His voice was low, carrying just far enough that the bench behind him went briefly quiet—meant only for me.

I didn't look up. I couldn't.

He stepped closer—but still didn't touch. Someone further down the bench shifted to make room without looking up. The air tightened, my skin aware of the path he moved through.

"You're safe." Barely more than a breath. The words brushed my skin before they reached my ears, settling somewhere lower.

He didn't move away.

I waited for my body to reject the words the way it always used to.

My shoulders stayed loose. My breath didn't lock.

"You don't have to hide from me."

He never explained himself, and somehow that restraint felt steadier than reassurance. It should have bothered me. In another life, it would have.

"Everyone came for the heat. I'm the only one watching you." His voice wrapped around me.

That should have unsettled me. But it didn't. He wasn't asking me to believe anything. Only to decide.

He wasn't claiming me or cornering me. He just stood there, patient, as if whatever happened next belonged to me. Waiting to see what I chose.

Another wave of eucalyptus rolled across the hall as the Meister swung his towel. The air moved like weather.

People groaned with pleasure. A few eyes flicked toward him before returning to the heat.

Steam shimmered around me like a veil, damp against my skin. My eyes stung with more than heat. I had to sit. Protocol. Standing made me exposed.

"Towel down," I whispered to myself. No one was forcing this. Not the heat. Not him. Not Tiinná.

The wood was hot beneath my feet. Dry heat. Solid. Real.

My hands trembled as I lifted the towel. For one suspended second, it hovered between us.

His gaze didn't shift. It held me there.

Then I let it fall.

No one gasped.

The room stayed exactly as before, but my pulse hammered so hard my throat ached.

Rurik's breath changed. Not louder. Deeper. Slower. His gaze moved over me slowly—not assessing, not consuming—but learning, as if committing each line to memory.

My arms lifted instinctively to cover myself, but Rurik raised his hands—gentle, calming. Reverent.

"Please." His hand lifted slowly—just hovering in the heat between us, steady enough that the air itself seemed to pause. Close enough that I felt his presence without contact. Close enough that the space between skin and skin felt charged.

He could have closed that distance.

He didn't.

"Don't hide," he murmured, like the thought had been waiting for me.

"Okay." I managed to murmur.

He stepped closer until only inches separated us, close enough that my body leaned toward him without permission. "You fought. I can see that." His gaze dropped to the vines. The words weren't sympathy. They sounded like recognition.

Something traced the ink from wrist to spine, as if a finger had followed a path that already existed.

Steam rose from the stones—and from somewhere deeper beneath it. It had to be the eucalyptus. The sweat. The adrenaline thick in my veins. It had to be something ordinary.

His gaze lingered on the ink.

"You feel that."

I searched his face for theatrics. For the thrill of saying something impossible.

There was none.

Rurik's breath left him in a broken exhale, trembling with something I couldn't name. Awe. Fear. Both.

"What are you saying?" I blinked.

He shook his head once, as if steadying himself.

"You survived something that should have ended you. And whatever woke up with you hasn't gone back to sleep."

From the top row, Tiinná looked down—saw the faint light pulsing beneath my ribs and the hunger in Rurik's eyes—and grinned like the matchmaker she was born to be.

His gaze scanned the hall and then returned to me.

"Shall we live in the frozen north or the sunny south?" Rurik intertwined his fingers with mine as I finally sat. The line should have been a joke. Instead, it felt like a lifeline.

"Excuse me?" I dragged my gaze up, the what-ifs flooding my mind.

I wasn't afraid of what he meant. I was afraid of how much I wanted to find out. Wanting wasn't the same as giving in. I had boundaries. I knew where they were.

"A poem. An ancient Norse myth. Not everything needs to be believed to be true." The words sounded less like explanation and more like something remembered. The corners of his mouth lifted.

There it was again. He smiled as if he'd answered me and hadn't. I could have pressed him, but I didn't.

Because whatever he was holding back felt contained. And because, for the first time in years, my body wasn't bracing for harm. It was listening.

I let that be enough.

"You read poetry?" My gaze drifted lower before I could stop it—nestled in a forest of golden curls, framed by thick, powerful thighs. Good God. Sex-starved for too long, I craved what I'd missed.

"Sagas. Myths. Legends." Each word rolled off his tongue with that delicious lilt.

"You mean fairy tales?" I pinched my lips together.

"I don't read fiction," he murmured, unbothered. "I read what lasts." His eyes crinkled when he smiled.

That wasn't an explanation. I let it stand anyway.

My gaze drifted over his chest. Ink marked him everywhere. Every line looked intentional.

And what of last night—and all those promises made? He'd had me at *kveldsmat*. I'd always been a sucker for a good diner.

"And what? Sagas and myths aren't fiction?" My belly fluttered.

He turned my hand slowly, as if asking permission without speaking. His thumb traced the center of my palm —once—and I answered. The heat that followed had nothing to do with the stones.

I didn't pull away. That was my choice.

And suddenly the room felt smaller.

"You look different with no clothes on," I said, half to myself.

The urge to laugh bubbled inside me. I couldn't stop smiling. Had I lost my mind? How had I gone from a dull workaholic to a sex-starved seductress in the span of twenty-four hours? This wasn't desperation. It was hunger.

"Did I make you laugh?" Desire shifted low in him—visible, unapologetic.

He didn't look away.

Damn.

"Tiinná said you were well-endowed. So, fill me in. What realm do you come from?" I glanced up at the rows of benches and spotted Tiinná waving from the highest perch.

"You know the Viking legends?" His skin glistened, every muscle and golden hair etched in heat and shadow.

"Hmm… You wear your stories on the outside, for all the world to see." My voice sounded strange to my own ears—bolder. Not the woman I'd been even yesterday.

The gong girl connected her phone to a wireless speaker, filling the heated cabin with the haunting strains of music.

"Tell me more." His voice tugged at heartstrings I didn't know I had.

At the center of his chest, black lines radiated from a single point—sharp, symmetrical.

"That one looks like it could start a war," I said softly.

His eyes lifted to mine before he answered.

"It's older than war."

His thumb pressed once into the center of my palm.

Over his heart, ink twisted into a knot so intricate I couldn't find where it began or ended.

"That one," I murmured. "That feels… permanent."

"Some things are."

Fire flicked along my inner thighs. Heat rose to my face. Betrayed by my own need. My throat closed as I tried to breathe.

"Tell me, Cristabel, what makes your heart thunder?" He drew circles on my palm, sending an electric charge through each digit.

"Thunder? Hmm…okay. Sleeping in. Walking in the forest. Chocolate. I'm not that complicated. What about you?" I tried to ignore the pulsing ache. I failed. God, I wanted to touch him.

"Meeting you yesterday made the top of my list." The words settled somewhere deep, like they'd been waiting longer than a day.

His crooked smile stirred something half-remembered. More sensation than image. His voice. I closed my eyes and drew in a breath, unable to still the pounding.

His gaze sharpened, not alarmed—focused. "Did something disturb you?"

His question pulled me out of the mist.

"I slept like a baby, although I had a dream." Doubt crept up my spine. How did I move past the demons?

How did I get on with my life? But I had. I was already there. Wasn't I?

"A dream?" His thumb paused.

"There was a rainbow." I edited myself without thinking. Sweat poured from every pore, every inch of my body —panic and lust tangled so tightly I couldn't tell them apart.

Rurik didn't look away, and neither did I.

He didn't rush me.

The dragon along his shoulder flexed when he inhaled, scales shifting with muscle. For a moment, I couldn't tell where ink ended, and something else began. I had the strangest sense it was watching me.

"Does it always look like that?"

His gaze shifted to my face. "Like what?"

"Like it's alive."

For a heartbeat, something shuttered behind his eyes. Not surprise. Recognition.

He didn't look at the dragon.

He looked at me.

Then his attention drifted toward the Aufgussmeister as if the timing had simply changed. His thumb never stopped tracing my palm.

"Are you going to the pub tonight?" he asked.

A young man in a sauna skirt explained the rules, ending with the most important: we could leave whenever we wished.

"The pub? For Tiinná's party? Of course."

The gong girl placed snowballs infused with essential oils onto the hot coals. She scooped water from a wooden bucket. The rocks hissed and sizzled as water struck them, the sound filling the room like rain on stone.

"I would like to accompany you."

I knew exactly what he wanted.

And worse—I wanted it too.

"You don't say anything by accident, do you?"

His mouth curved. "No."

The crowd ooh'ed and ahh'ed as the Meister swirled his towel in helicopter arcs, sending hot air currents our way. His movements synchronized with the lyrical music as he narrated a story to his entranced audience.

"What's he saying?" I inched closer, catching Rurik's heated gaze one more time.

"He's telling the Christmas story of the *julenisse*," he leaned closer, his voice dropping low enough that it belonged only to me, his cooling breath grazing the back of my neck.

"What's a *julenisse*?" My voice tripped over the frog in my throat, floating downriver on a raft of lust—with Rurik as my boatman.

"A *julenisse* is a magical creature who lives in the forest." He said it like a story, not a warning. He lingered, teasing my earlobe with a soft nibble.

"Oh... another fairy tale?" My breath caught, and the ache deepened. I took a deep breath, captivated by the Meister's towel dance and Rurik's closeness.

Whatever Rurik believed, he wasn't pulling me forward. He was walking beside me—matching pace, watching for my hesitation.

The gong girl walked among the guests, offering fist-sized snowballs by the bucketful. Rurik took two.

"Are you ready?" He waited for my breath to catch.

Waited for my nod.

Only then did he lift the ice to my skin, slow enough that I felt the air move first. The cold bit instantly.

The first touch stole the air from my lungs.

I noticed then—how his every movement paused until I answered first. The pace wasn't his. It was mine.

"Ooh, that's wonderful." I dropped my head, lost in the burning contrast of melting ice and his fingertips moving through the water, drawing familiar patterns on my skin.

The Meister finished with a final swirl of his towel, the fabric cracking softly in the steam, reminding everyone to shower before entering the cold pools.

As the heat faded, the awareness didn't.

The cold pools wouldn't change what had already started.

The heat didn't leave.

It just changed shape.

Somehow, he was still at the center of it.

15

INTO THE ABYSS

Cristabel

He clasped my elbow and drew me forward. For a fraction of a second, I thought we were simply weaving through the steam and tiled corridors toward the showers.

Then the floor shifted beneath my feet.

The warmth that had wrapped around my skin thinned and broke apart, unravelling into air so cold it caught in my throat. The scent of eucalyptus dissolved, replaced by pine sap and river water and something metallic and clean that didn't belong indoors.

I blinked against the sting.

Snow lay where the sauna door should be. Trees stood in its place, dark trunks rising straight into a pale winter sky. My breath left me in a white ribbon, curling between us before fading.

I didn't ask how it was possible.

My palms flattened against him—seeking more than balance. His skin burned compared to the air, and the contrast sent a slow, electric awareness across my breasts and down my spine. He shuddered when my nipples brushed his chest—subtle, controlled, unmistakable. A small sound left him. Barely there. Not imagined.

Somewhere ahead, water roared.

It was not distant. It lived in the air around us, thrumming through my ribs as if the earth itself were breathing hard.

On the far bank of a silvered pool, reindeer lowered their heads to drink from the river's edge. Their coats were thick and pale against the snow, steam rising from their flanks. One lifted its antlered head slowly, its dark eyes sliding over us without alarm, as though we were not intruders but part of something already accounted for.

The antlers framed the pale sky like a crown.

"Look," I murmured, my voice small against the landscape.

Rurik's hand settled over my wrist, his palm warm against my cooling skin. His thumb pressed lightly into the pulse, grounding me.

"Animals notice what moves beneath the surface." His breath brushed my temple.

I did not challenge him. The words didn't feel like either performance or warning. They felt like observation.

He lowered his chin to the crown of my head, the rhythm of his heart steady against my spine. His fingers traced down my shoulders and along my arms, coaxing warmth back into my skin with patient touches that deepened my breath.

He didn't rush the contact. His thumbs pressed lightly into the insides of my elbows, then slid back up again, mapping me as though reacquainting himself with something long familiar. The slowness unravelled me faster than urgency ever could.

"You say strange things." My protest lacked conviction. Heat was already returning, not from embarrassment, not from fear, but from somewhere lower and more insistent.

"I have waited a long time to meet you like this." His mouth grazed the curve of my ear, unhurried, certain, as though time itself had bent to accommodate us.

"Naked?" I tilted my face up toward his. "You could have had me last night."

"You were sleeping." His thumb skimmed my cheekbone and lingered there. "I left Odin with you."

The name should have unsettled me. Instead, I felt the echo of something protective in it, like a sentry placed at a door I hadn't realized was still vulnerable.

Snow loosened from a branch overhead and drifted onto my shoulders, melting instantly against overheated skin.

My hands moved on their own, sliding down the firm heat of his chest, feeling the flex and release of muscle beneath my palms.

He didn't guide them. He let me explore. Let me decide. The trust in that restraint tightened something low in my belly.

I followed the pale line of curls downward, slower now, aware of the cold biting my shoulders, weight thickening in my palm. When my fingers finally closed around him, I squeezed—slow and sure—feeling the full length of him.

His lips parted then stilled. Not shock. Control.

I stroked once, testing the length of him, the heat, the tension drawn tight beneath my grip. His hips answered before he could stop them—barely a shift forward, just enough that the pressure deepened.

His jaw tightened, but he did not step back.

My hand slid higher, thumb dragging upward, tracing the ridge of him before circling back down again, firmer this time.

A rough exhale escaped him. His fingers flexed at my waist—then stilled.

He was letting me do this.

He was choosing to.

"Are you always this bold?" His voice roughened, but he didn't retreat.

"Only when I know I won't be overpowered."

His gaze darkened. "You won't be."

Not a promise.

Fact.

He drew me closer by the nape of my neck, not roughly, not urgently—just enough that my spine curved toward him without resistance. His mouth brushed mine once, testing, his lips warm and firm against the cold.

The second kiss didn't linger.

His mouth opened over mine without hurry—without retreat. The cold slipped between us—and then vanished.

I held him one heartbeat longer.

Then I let go.

My fingers slid up the length of him as they released, easing their grip inch by deliberate inch.

A low sound escaped him—unhidden this time.

Only then did my hands travel upward, over the hard plane of his abdomen, over his chest, until my fingers curled into his shoulders, nails grazing skin as if I needed to anchor him there.

He tasted warm, clean, faintly metallic with river mist.

His tongue brushed my lower lip, asking. I opened for him, breath catching as warmth melted the frost gathered along my shoulders. The contrast was dizzying—winter biting at my back while his mouth claimed warmth from mine.

My hands moved across his chest, fingers splaying wide. I needed to anchor myself to something solid. His skin was hot, almost fevered, compared to the air. When my thumbs grazed his nipples, he inhaled sharply, the sound low and restrained.

He deepened the kiss without overpowering it. His tongue stroked, retreated, returned again.

My knees softened. My belly tightened. The space between my thighs throbbed with a pulse that matched the rhythm of the waterfall behind us.

My teeth caught his lower lip.

Not accidentally.

I bit down. Not enough to wound. Enough to test.

His hand tightened in my hair just enough to make my scalp sting. His control was a choice.

When he broke the kiss, he did not pull away. He rested his forehead against mine, breath mingling, his hand sliding from my neck down the curve of my spine until his palm settled at the small of my back.

He held me there. Not claiming. Steadying.

Above us, a raven split the sky with a harsh cry. Its wings beat once, then twice, before the sound stretched thin and dissolved into the roar of the river.

He studied my face as if committing it to memory.

"Do you like what you see?"

I let my gaze travel over him openly, taking in the

breadth of his shoulders, the strength in his thighs, the rise and fall of his chest.

"A girl could lose her way here." I pressed my palm flat against his sternum and felt the firm, solid thud beneath.

"And what would she be searching for?" His thumb returned to the center of my palm, tracing the same slow circle. The sensation travelled up my arm and settled low in my belly, heavy and bright.

My fingers traced lower, over the ridge of muscle and the subtle flex beneath my touch. My palm moved with intent, feeling the weight of him before I closed my hand.

He was hot. Heavy. Fully awake.

His breath changed when my fingers tightened—not louder but deeper, as if he were drawing air from somewhere farther down in his lungs. His hips shifted almost imperceptibly toward me, testing the pressure without taking it.

I stroked him once, watching his throat work as he swallowed.

His hand slid into my hair, not pulling, just gathering it loosely at the base of my skull. His thumb brushed behind my ear, and that small touch—so tender compared to the boldness of what I held—sent a sharper surge through me than anything else.

Snow melted along my collarbones. Cold air brushed my breasts, tightening my nipples into aching points.

His gaze dropped there openly. He didn't smirk. Didn't tease. He dragged his knuckles across my nipples slowly enough that I felt the air before the heat—then pressure.

My body jerked.

He saw it.

He did it again.

He watched the way my mouth parted, the way my pulse jumped in my throat.

"You're not pretending anymore." His tone felt less like praise and more like recognition.

I tightened my grip.

I used him.

Not gently.

I stroked him harder, slower, feeling the drag of skin and heat and the undeniable pulse that answered me.

"Careful." His jaw flexed.

Not a warning.

A promise.

His composure fractured—not completely—but enough.

His hips pressed forward fully this time, forcing the friction, the glide of my hand over him.

My thumb dragged along the underside of him before sliding upward, watching his control thin. His eyes closed briefly, and a low sound escaped him—uncontrolled, honest.

The river thundered. Or maybe it was just the blood in my ears.

I dragged him closer by the nape this time, claiming the kiss instead of waiting for it. My mouth opened against his.

He answered in kind.

His tongue slid deeper, slower, claiming the space I gave him and taking just a little more.

His hand tightened in my hair, tipping my head back enough that the cold air struck my throat while his mouth devoured mine.

His grip traced down my spine and cupped me fully, fingers digging into the curve of my hip hard enough that I felt the mark of him there.

Behind him, the trees parted to reveal a wall of ice and stone where water hurled itself downward in a relentless sheet. Mist rose in thick plumes, clinging to my lashes and freezing in the ends of my hair. The roar swallowed the edges of thought.

I had built my life on restraint.

My body refused it.

Standing there, naked in the snow with his hand still firm at my back, I understood what frightened me was not the water.

He pressed his mouth to mine again, deeper now, less restrained. His hips aligned with mine, the warmth solid and undeniable between us. I could have taken him there —snow, river, sky watching.

The thought didn't scare me. It steadied me.

What frightened me was stepping back.

"The waterfall?" I asked, though the word felt small compared to the force before us.

He did not answer immediately. He stepped closer until our bodies fit, skin against skin, his warmth pressing into my cold. His breath moved steadily against my temple, grounding me in the present.

"Whatever happens." His voice was nearly lost in the thunder of water. "Do not let go."

Mist thickened around us, clinging to my lashes and settling against my breasts like a second skin. My hair stiffened at the ends where droplets froze into tiny crystals. Every nerve sharpened.

He stepped behind me.

I let him.

His chest pressed to my back, heat enveloping me from behind while cold spray struck my front.

For a flicker of a second, the pressure of him behind me shifted. Not lover. Not only that. A body braced at my back against a storm.

My spine straightened instinctively, as though I were standing on moving wood instead of stone, wind ripping past my ears while water struck the hull hard enough to rattle bone.

The falls thundered.

The river carried a trace of salt.

His heartbeat stumbled once against my spine before finding its rhythm again. His fingers flexed once at my waist, tightening as though the shift in the air had reached him, too.

His arms circled my waist and held—firm now. Not guiding. Holding.

The familiarity of it tightened my throat.

This did not feel new. It felt remembered.

His mouth found the curve of my shoulder. Deliberate—unhurried, intentional. He pressed a kiss there, open-mouthed, slow enough that I felt the warmth of his breath before the heat of his tongue.

My spine arched without permission.

The vines beneath my skin pulsed once—soft, luminous beneath the surface—then quieted, as though listening.

His hands moved once—up, then down—slow, measured, as if confirming I was real.

"Feel the cold," he murmured against my skin. "Let it take your breath."

His hand slid between my thighs from behind.

He stilled there.

I rolled my hips back into his palm, and ground against him—slow, deliberate—letting winter bite while pressure built between us.

His breath broke against my neck.

"Cristabel."

This time, not recognition.

Need.

His fingers pressed into the slickness already gathered.

I was wet.

Achingly so.

And he felt it.

The roar below us swelled and subsided in a heavy rhythm, and I responded—not with fear or hesitation but with the same grounding I had with my feet firmly planted on a pitching deck.

The memory did not arrive in images this time. It arrived in stance. In the rhythm of breathing. In the refusal to step back.

My head fell back against his shoulder.

The waterfall thundered below us, and yet the loudest sound in my body was the rush of heat between my legs.

His hand did not waver, patient enough that my body had to decide first.

My hips shifted first. A sound broke from me—low, involuntary.

His breath left him rough against my neck.

"Cristabel."

Not warning.

Knowing.

Spray struck my face in sharp bursts, cold enough to

steal breath, yet I felt something under my skin stir in response—not flare, not blaze, but hum, as though recognizing the rhythm of the falling water. For a moment the mist seemed to hesitate around us, as if the river itself were deciding whether to claim or release what stood at its edge.

He stood with me at the edge, as though waiting for something.

I leaned forward.

His grip tightened—not stopping me.

Matching me.

For one heartbeat, his hand slid lower, fingers almost breaching the line between restraint and possession.

He caught himself.

Not because he had to.

Because he chose to.

His hand held mine. Steady. Certain.

Mist struck my face. I didn't flinch. My body leaned forward into it the way it had once leaned into salt spray and storm wind.

If the river wanted me, it would have to fight him for me.

And I wasn't sure which of us it should fear more.

This is not the day we die.

The river roared.

So did I.

Not aloud. But inside my blood.

I stepped forward.

And he followed.

16

THE FOURTH LIFE

Cristabel

The cold struck first.

As if the river had closed around us.

Not the clean sting of winter air, but a weight that folded around my ribs and pressed inward until my lungs forgot how to expand. A heartbeat later, the sound followed—water hammering stone, relentless and unbroken, loud enough to jar something old loose in my spine.

My shoulders tightened before I gave them permission. My breath shortened on its own. Whatever moved inside me recognized this place before I did.

"Rurik, what are we doing here?" The words thinned in the spray, swallowed almost as soon as they left me.

He let the question hang between us. Snow spiralled around us while he drew me closer to the falling curtain.

Beneath my ribs, the vines strained outward—not hot, not painful, just insistent, like something testing the limits of skin it no longer fit. Moonlight fractured in the spray, turning everything silver and unreal.

"Stop." I caught his wrist, harder than I intended. "Something's wrong."

He turned toward me, and for a second the noise seemed to drop away. His gaze wasn't startled. It wasn't confused. It was calm in a way that made my pulse spike harder.

"Nothing is wrong," he told me, voice low enough that I felt it more than heard it. "Not today."

His hand slid from my wrist to lace through my fingers, his palm warm against my numbing skin. He did not tug. He waited.

I didn't know why I believed him.

But I did.

The water hit like impact—heat and ice at once, shock snapping through my nerves until my knees trembled. My hair plastered to my back. The old scars along my ribs tightened in the cold, skin pulling thin and bright.

Then the ink stirred.

The vines traced over the scar tissue like dark roots laid across stone, and heat moved along those lines—not under them, not separate from them—but through the places where skin had once split and healed wrong.

The warmth didn't stay on the surface. It sank inward, threading through the scar tissue until the tightest places in me began to loosen under its touch.

The air tightened. Not colder—closer.

I flattened my palm against the stone to steady myself and felt, unmistakably, that the rock was thinner than it should have been, like a second layer lay just beneath the surface, waiting for skin.

Lines sharpened under the sheet of water. Curves and angles revealed themselves in the flow, carvings worn smooth by centuries of impact. My vision narrowed before I could stop it. My tongue pressed against my teeth, straining toward a word lodged just out of reach.

Astrid.

The name struck like swallowed salt.

Solveig.

My pulse staggered.

For a moment, the waterfall shifted. Not river—ocean.

Wind tore across my face. Salt stung my eyes raw. The deck pitched beneath my feet, and I braced without thinking—feet planted wide, knees bent, body remembering the stance, as black water climbed the hull and broke over us in blinding spray.

Men shouted into a sky split by storm.

Oars drove hard.

The mast groaned above me.

My hand was wrapped around another hand—firm, unyielding, steady through the surge.

Hold.

The sea snapped back into river.

Cold returned—stone, mist, the river's ceaseless thunder.

My knees gave out.

Rurik caught me before the ground could, his hands sliding up my arms, gripping just hard enough to anchor without bruising. He pulled me close, chest to chest, heat pouring from him into the cold space between us. His mouth brushed my temple—not a kiss, not yet. Contact. Breath. Presence.

"Easy." His voice brushed my ear.

He stayed like that.

Breathing with me.

Matching my inhale until it lengthened. Matching my exhale until the shaking eased, until my pulse followed it down from panic to something steadier.

"Why are they doing that?" My voice scraped thin in the spray.

His hand slid lower, hovering over my sternum but not touching. He knew where the heat was gathering.

"They're responding."

The word landed wrong.

"To what?"

His jaw set before he spoke. "To you."

Light moved inside the falling water, faint and submerged, as though the river carried its own pulse.

"I'm hallucinating." I shook my head.

He turned me fully toward him, his palms framing my shoulders, thumbs pressing lightly as though testing whether I was still solid. "Stay with me." His forehead nearly touched mine. "Look at me."

I tried. I truly did. But something shifted behind the falling veil. A density in the spray. A presence too large for the chamber to contain.

My fingers dug into his arms. The air tasted metallic, sharp.

Then a black butterfly drifted down through the spray and settled on my palm.

Everything inside me stilled.

The pressure eased instantly, as if whatever had been rising paused to watch it too.

My breath slowed.

Rurik's gaze moved from the butterfly to my face and back again. There was no performance in him now. No teasing. Just a depth that unsettled me more than the runes had.

We stepped through the curtain together.

The roar dulled the moment we crossed the threshold, as though the water became a wall instead of a sound. The chamber beyond opened slowly, stone slick underfoot, air cool and thick. Roots thrust through the rock at the center, pale and faintly luminous, pushing through stone like bone through flesh.

The vines beneath my skin surged in answer.

Runes spiralled outward from the roots, carved in concentric rings that breathed as I moved closer. I reached without meaning to, my fingers brushing one glowing line.

The contact answered my touch, as if the stone remembered skin.

"Eldr." The word formed on its own. Fire.

The rune flared brighter.

Another line woke.

fjórði.

Fourth.

The sound of it hollowed my lungs.

The space tilted.

For a suspended instant, the chamber dissolved around me. The roar of the waterfall warped into something wider, wilder. Not river—sea. Wind tore across my face so fiercely I tasted salt. My hands were wrapped around a carved helm slick with brine, knuckles white, muscles braced as the deck pitched violently beneath my feet.

Men shouted into a sky ripped open by storm. The wind howled. Oars drove hard through black water. The mast groaned above me. A wave rose high enough to blot out sky. The deck heaved.

And beside me—

Rurik.

Not as he stood now, bare and golden in the cave's pale glow, but armoured in salt and iron, his hand wrapped around mine with the same unyielding steadiness.

Hold.

The wave rose.

The ship climbed it.

The chamber snapped back into place with the violence of breath returning after submersion.

Cold stone under my feet. Mist in my lungs. Rurik at my shoulder.

His hand paused at my waist, as if completing the touch might change something, as though contact might tip whatever balance he was trying to maintain.

"You shouldn't read those." And though his voice was quiet, it carried weight.

"Why?" My voice trembled, but I held his gaze.

He swallowed, deciding how much to say. "Because they keep score."

It didn't feel like a promise. It felt older than that.

It felt carved—waiting for my skin.

More runes brightened slowly along the walls, their glow subtle at first, then undeniable.

rót.

The word brushed through me like roots pushing through dark soil.

seiðr.

It vibrated low in my sternum, old and feminine and dangerous.

konungr undir.

The syllables carried weight, heavy as something buried beneath stone.

The roots of the tree pulsed faintly, and beneath my skin the vines answered in sharp, brilliant heat that bordered on pain. It didn't tear me apart. It flooded me all at once, too sudden to dismiss.

The roar swelled in volume, as if the world outside the chamber were reclaiming its voice.

"One that keeps finding you."

The words met my fear before I could shape it into a question.

The glow extinguished as abruptly as it had risen. The vines throbbed once beneath my scars, then dimmed, retreating into my skin like embers banked for later.

The butterfly lifted from my palm and dissolved into mist.

The chamber exhaled.

Sound returned in full force.

My knees weakened gradually rather than collapsing outright, as if my body were carefully powering down. Rurik caught me before gravity completed the job, one arm sliding beneath my thighs, the other securing my back. He drew me close enough that my cheek pressed to the steady plane of his chest, and for a moment his forehead rested against mine in a quiet gesture that felt less romantic than reverent.

He did not speak.

His grip was careful—too careful. Not instinct alone, but control layered over something tighter beneath the surface.

His thumb traced the edge of my ribs and stopped just

short of where the vines had flared brightest. He knew exactly where the line was. That small hesitation told me more than any explanation.

Even through the haze creeping into my vision, I felt the shift in him.

Whatever moved behind his eyes wasn't panic. It was assessment—quiet, controlled, already thinking ahead.

His breath hitched once before smoothing out, and I understood that whatever had awakened in the stone had not surprised him entirely. Only the timing had.

The cold began to recede as he carried me back through the curtain of water, mist striking his shoulders and sliding down over us both. Darkness closed in slowly, not as panic but as heaviness.

Yet the pressure in my chest did not fade.

It settled there, low and persistent, no longer flaring but no longer dormant either—like a bruise forming beneath the skin, waiting to surface when pressed.

I did not ask him what he knew.

I did not have the strength.

But even as the world dimmed and his heartbeat steadied against my ear, I understood something I could not yet articulate:

This felt chosen.

And beneath his calm, he was already standing against it.

17

AFTER THE AWAKENING

C*ristabel*

"I almost fell through something." My voice shook. "What was that?"

A whisper moved beneath my skin.

"A reaction." His calm didn't match the storm moving through my body. "To the heat. The cold. To the day."

He didn't meet my eyes when he said it. Not avoidance. He held himself steady, matching my breathing instead of overtaking it. The explanation dissolved before I could grab it.

"You forgot lightning. And ancient runes. And whatever tried to crawl into my lungs." I arched a brow. "Is that included in the package?"

"And something else," he added, quieter now. "Something I don't entirely command."

I blinked, my eyelids heavy.

"Cristabel." He brushed my cheek with his thumb, careful, reverent. "We should get you warm."

I nodded. Dazed. Trembling.

But as he led me away, one truth haunted the back of my mind. I hadn't imagined it. My body felt altered. Less guarded. Sensation moved through me without hesitation, without flinching first. The waterfall's roar was replaced by the crackle of fire, soft hides—dun-coloured reindeer skins. Embers burst, sending blue spirals up the stone chimney and beyond the mullioned windows, fingers of mist curling over a black forest.

The fire snapped once as if it had heard something it didn't like. A log shifted in the hearth with a hollow crack, and for a fleeting second, my senses tingled.

Then it passed.

The next thing I knew, there was firelight and fur under my back. No darkness. No absence. I remembered falling —and then being caught. The scent of wintergreen and smoke. The roar of the waterfall imprinted in my mind, and the cold.

"Are you all right?" Rurik lay beside me, his head propped on his hand. Bare-chested, muscles sculpted, skin golden, dark jeans hugging his hips—buttoned and snug.

Something about it felt wrong. Or right in the most impossible way.

"What are you? A sorcerer? A male witch? I saw things. I heard voices. Do you carry a staff? A secret spell book? Should I be checking for horns?" My lips twitched even as my pulse fluttered.

I didn't mean it as an accusation.

"What did the voices say?" His blue eye sparked.

"I don't know. It's a blur. A beautiful blur." I stretched beneath him, lengthening muscles, wiggling toes, testing this new, humming body.

"*Hmm.*" He offered no answers. Instead, he slid down.

I checked for fear. It didn't answer.

What answered instead was a quiet certainty—like my body recognized him as part of the ground beneath my feet.

His breath moved over me, warming. He traced the inside of my thigh with his knuckles instead of his mouth.

I shifted, impatient.

He didn't reward it. His lips brushed my hipbone instead. Then lower. Then away again.

"You're cruel," I whispered.

His mouth curved. "You're rushing."

"If you're going to stare at it," I murmured, sliding my fingers into his hair and tightening slightly, "you should probably do something about it."

My hips rolled once—inviting, not pleading.

The anticipation tightened until even the fire felt too far away.

His hand flattened over my stomach and held me there. Not denying me—just making me wait.

He lowered his mouth slowly—like he meant to take his time with me. When his tongue touched me, he exhaled into me first—a slow breath that made my hips lift before he even moved. Then he pressed in with deliberate pressure, circling once before settling into a rhythm that felt practiced rather than exploratory.

The first stroke unravelled me.

Not gently.

Completely.

The fire cracked in the hearth. The fur beneath my shoulders shifted, coarse against my skin as my body tightened.

The sound felt wrong against my skin.

His exhale warmed me more than the fire did. Slow. Controlled.

A flicker of salt wind crossed my tongue.

This wasn't here. It wasn't now.

But it was mine.

Each stroke shifted something inside me—tight muscle giving way, breath shortening, my hands gripping harder into the fur. I could no longer remember where my body ended, and the wanting began.

His hand tightened once in the fur beneath me. As if he needed something solid to hold onto.

I tipped my head back, the warmth rising. I broke then—a sharp cry torn from my throat as the pleasure tightened low and snapped outward, leaving my thighs trembling and my vision washed white for a breath too long.

"Come apart for me." His voice dropped, rough and low. "Let me feel what you are."

I didn't soften. I didn't retreat. I dragged him up by the hair and kissed him hard, tasting myself on his mouth.

Beyond our nest, a massage table waited, stocked with oils. A luxe bag with the spa logo sat near a chair. Our clothing—the ones we'd arrived in folded neatly. Our footwear sat on a warming rack by the door.

A grin shaped his mouth when he pulled back. When his gaze dropped again, something low and electric moved through me.

"There was a wolf between two rowan trees. He was watching. And a butterfly," I managed, writhing as his tongue worked me closer and closer to the edge, each stroke finding its mark.

The image rose whole. Not hazy. Not distant. Close enough to taste.

As if my body knew before my mind did.

"The wolf watches," he breathed against me. "Doesn't mean he gets invited in." He shifted, leaning over me, coarse denim rasping my tender skin, the only thing separating his thickness from my need.

"The waterfall isn't just a waterfall," I whispered. The air *buzzed* on my tongue, like I was tasting electricity. "Where did you take me?"

"Into where you've stood before." His mouth set into a hard line as if he'd already said too much.

His gaze flicked away before I could press him.

"That's not comforting," I murmured. "That sounds like something a man says right before a ritual sacrifice."

His fingers tightened on my hip without him seeming to notice.

The dragon along his shoulder flexed as he moved—ink bending with muscle—and for a second it looked almost alive. Or maybe that was just the way he held himself.

I blinked. It was still.

Had I imagined it?

"The past? What do you mean?" I gripped his shoulders, desperate to hold onto something.

His hand stilled.

For a heartbeat, something unguarded flickered across his face. Not confusion. Not fear. Just grief.

"I mean," he began, and stopped. "Do you know how much I've missed this?" He smiled, wicked and tender all at once. His hand skimmed lower, lifting my bottom to meet his hunger.

"What do you mean? You could have any number of

ladies in this town." I poked his shoulder with my finger, my breath leaving me.

"You weren't supposed to remember." His thumb pressed into the hollow of my throat as if feeling for something that had once rested there.

"Remember what?"

"This." His thumb traced the line of my collarbone, buying himself time.

I studied him. "You keep answering the wrong question."

His mouth curved. "Do I?"

"Yes. And you're very good at it."

"I want to taste you. I need to taste you." He planted one hand on my hip, the other lifting my knee, opening me to his delving tongue, sending a surge through me that arched my back off the floor.

His breath went uneven—not from exertion, but from holding himself back.

"Yes—don't stop." My voice broke as the pleasure crested again, spreading outward in slow, rolling waves that made my fingers tighten in his hair.

"Again," I whispered against his lips. "I'm not fragile."

His eyes darkened—not surprised. Waiting for me to ask.

I spread my arms across the floor, lost in the lazy strokes of his tongue. The tight center of me throbbed, swollen and hungry.

"Yes, do that." My hand flattened at the back of his neck, holding him there as pulsing sensations cascaded through me. My breath left me before I could stop it.

"You don't understand what this costs." He lingered

longer than control allowed. His fingers dug in harder than he meant.

When he pulled back, it cost him.

"You keep saying that like I'm signing a contract." My voice came out breathless. "Am I agreeing to something?"

His tongue slowed. "You already did."

Not because he was finished—but because something outside the walls had shifted.

My hands tightened in his hair. "Then tell me."

He stilled.

My body arched, chasing friction that wasn't there.

The space between strokes felt crueller than the touch itself. Every pause stretched thin. He held me at the edge.

"Look at me." He waited until I did.

Only then did he lower his mouth, pressing harder instead of answering.

My thighs trembled around his shoulders from the steadiness of him. He didn't rush. He adjusted—slower when I tensed, firmer when I arched.

I tasted smoke. Salt. Him.

"Cristabel." He dipped his head, his mouth closing over my clitoris. Lapping. Suckling. Kneading my bottom with all five fingers, he brought me to the edge again, every nerve ending flared at once.

Outside the cabin door, boots stomped—voices rose in conversation. Someone giggled. I knew that giggle.

"Someone's coming." He caged me in his arms.

"That was me." I giggled as aftershocks raced through me. "You started this." My voice was wrecked. I pinched his chin and licked his mouth. I wanted more.

"I like making you come." He didn't smile when he said it. "I like the sounds you make. You purr like a satisfied cat." He traced my stomach, fingers carving a slow path toward my still-aching sex. "I like knowing I'm the one who does that to you."

"Careful," I murmured, dragging my heel up the back of his thigh. "I might start expecting it."

"You should."

There was no teasing in that.

"Cristabel? Rurik? Are you in there?" Tiinná's voice filtered through the thick door, accompanied by the chiming bells that signalled the end of a session.

The fire snapped again.

This time it didn't sound like wood.

A tap sounded through the heavy door.

"Do we have to go?" I swallowed hard as Rurik crossed the room.

Broad shoulders. Narrow waist. Denim stretched tight across muscle.

A vision intruded—uninvited and vivid. Rurik, hair braided, leather strapped tight across his chest, silver catching firelight, astride a black stallion. A woman rode a white mare beside him, her snow-white hair streaming over a crimson cloak edged with gold, galloping across a barren, icy landscape, hooves thundering in my mind.

"Well, hello. Are you okay? Cristabel? Are you there? How was the massage?" Tiinná peeked around him, her grin wide, her eyes dancing.

"Hi, Tiinná." Heat flooded my face. I knew what she saw—my lips swollen from his kisses, my hair a tousled mess, the glow beneath my skin.

I wasn't ashamed. That surprised me most.

"Are you inviting me in?" A wintry gust slipped under the door.

I snuggled deeper into the fur rug, unwilling to surrender what I'd found, counting the times Tiinná had saved me from myself. Friends like that come once in a lifetime.

"Cristabel is busy." His hand stayed on the doorframe.

"Okay, well, it's checkout time, lover boy." She giggled, then lowered her voice. "Don't make her late."

The door clicked shut.

He stood there a moment longer than necessary. His hand closed once at his side.

His gaze flicked once toward the window. Toward the forest.

"Rurik?"

He turned back to me like a man walking away from a cliff. His shoulders were rigid. Not desire. Something colder.

For a second, the air in the cabin felt thinner—like something that had pressed close to the walls stepped back again. And when he looked at me, hunger wasn't what I saw first.

It was distance.

Then he crossed the room like a man who had already decided.

Rurik

She was watching me when I turned back, stretched across the furs as if she had never gone still in my arms at all.

I stood there longer than I should have, my hand

resting on the wood. Not because I didn't want her. I did. But because I needed to see her chest rise again.

Beneath the waterfall, for one suspended second, her body had gone slack in my arms. I knew that stillness. The terrible lightness that followed it. I had felt it before. Under different skies.

But this time she had opened her eyes and come back to me.

She tipped her head when she noticed the way I was watching her, that slow, wicked smile curving her mouth. "What?" Her fingers traced idle circles in the fur beside her. "You look like you've seen something you don't like."

I crossed the room carefully, as though sudden movement might disturb the mercy that had settled over us. The fire cracked behind her, sparks snapping upward. Outside, the forest stood dark beyond the mullioned windows, silent and waiting.

I lowered myself beside her and let my palm settle at her waist, warm and solid under my palm. When I bent and pressed my mouth just below her breast, her skin tightened.

"You frightened me."

She huffed a soft laugh and pushed her fingers into my hair. "You dragged me under a waterfall in December."

"I caught you."

"You did." Her hand tightened, not tender but claiming, guiding me where she wanted me. "I'm fine."

I let my forehead rest against her stomach and closed my eyes longer than pride allowed.

I had held her in three winters.

I had felt her grow cold.

I had walked away once because staying would have broken what little remained of me.

The memory pressed close, but I kept it buried beneath the heat of her skin.

"You're thinking," she accused lightly, tugging my hair until I looked up at her.

"I always am."

"Stop." Her heel dragged up the back of my thigh. "You're thinking too much."

I caught her ankle and pressed my mouth to the inside of it, grounding myself there. She flexed her toes, amused, testing me.

I slid back to her hip.

"Last I checked." She leaned up on her elbows, studying me more closely now. "I don't like it when you look at me like that."

"Like what?"

"Like I'm about to disappear."

My grip tightened. I made myself ease it, tracing slow circles along her skin instead. The firelight moved across her body in golden strokes, catching in her hair, along the curve of her collarbone.

"You won't." The words scraped on the way out.

She reached up and brushed her thumb along my jaw, slow and thoughtful, as if memorizing me in return. "I'm not going anywhere."

She had said that before. It changed nothing.

I bent and kissed her—not with urgency, not with hunger. Just the slow meeting of mouths. She opened for me immediately, heat blooming between us, her body arching into mine with the easy confidence of someone who did not expect to be taken away.

Hope slipped in before I could stop it.

She felt it. Of course she did. Her lips curved faintly against mine before she drew back an inch. "There it is." Her eyes searched mine. "That look again."

"What look?"

"The one where you almost tell me something."

I brushed my thumb over her lower lip instead of answering. Her pulse fluttered there. Alive. Present.

"If I start glowing again." Her brow lifted. "I expect at least a warning."

A laugh caught in my throat and escaped despite me. I dipped my head and kissed her again, deeper this time, letting my body speak where my mouth would not. My hand slid up her ribs, over her breast, down her waist, mapping her as if reacquainting myself with what I had once lost.

She rolled beneath me, guiding me over her, thighs parting without hesitation. "See?" She dragged her nails down my back. "Still here."

Still here. My chest tightened at her words.

I lowered myself over her fully, letting my weight settle slowly, careful not to fracture what couldn't be seen. She wrapped her legs around my hips, grounding me with the firm pressure of her heels at my back.

Her mouth moved against mine again, softer now, teasing. "You're allowed to be happy about it," she breathed.

Happy.

The word felt fragile.

I kissed her throat instead of answering, then the hollow beneath it, my hand splaying wide over her stomach to feel the rise of her breath again. She arched into the touch, impatient with my restraint.

"You're doing that thing," she accused, fingers sliding into my hair once more.

"What thing?"

"Touching me like I'm made of glass."

I stilled for half a heartbeat.

Then I pressed my palm more firmly into her hip, letting my thumb dig just enough to leave a mark. Her breath hitched—pleased.

"Better," she whispered.

She was here. Warm. Laughing. Defiant.

For the first time in longer than I dared measure, survival did not feel like borrowed time. It felt like a beginning.

And beginnings were always the most dangerous thing of all.

18

MEAD, MYTHS, AND MOUTHS

C*ristabel*

I sat at the edge of the bed with my robe undone and my hair damp from the steam, trying to convince my hands to stop shaking long enough to cooperate.

The room was quiet except for the tick-tick-tock of the old grandfather clock in the hall. The same clock that had sounded strange the night I arrived—like it kept time for something that didn't belong here.

Odin curled at my feet, a warm, purring loaf, blinking up at me.

I drew in a careful breath, and the scent of spruce, cold water, and Rurik filled my lungs so completely my balance shifted. My lips were tender. My skin still flushed. The inside of my thighs carried a dull, delicious ache that pulsed in time with memory.

Beneath the warmth and lingering pleasure, something opened inside me, and did not feel inclined to close.

Desire alone did not explain the tremor under my ribs.

I knew desire. I trusted it. What unsettled me was everything that came before it—the moment under the falling water when the world had narrowed and widened at once as if waiting for me.

I pressed a hand to my chest, to the vines etched there, pulsing under my palm—one soft glow, like a lightning bug trapped under my skin.

"Don't start."

They started anyway. A slow wave radiated through my ribs, weaving outward like fingertips tracing the inked vines.

The waterfall's roar echoed in my ears. Colours shifted through the spray—impossible colours. The shape behind the water too large to be a rock. And the butterfly. God, the butterfly.

I shivered, pulling the robe tighter. The room was warm, but the memory chilled me. When it landed on my palm, the world had stopped—like roots beneath the earth reaching up to brush my skin, slow and patient.

"I don't believe in omens." My voice thinned.

Odin flicked an ear, unimpressed.

I stood and paced to the window, wiping the condensation with my sleeve. Snow fell in fat flakes, drifting lazily past the lamplight. The town looked peaceful. Ordinary. Real. So why didn't I feel real?

I lifted my wrist to my nose. I still smelled of waterfall spray and Rurik's hands, even after my shower. My lips tingled where he'd kissed me beneath that thundering curtain of white. My hips still bore the imprint of his fingers. But under all that physical sensation, a whisper. A hum. A trembling thread pulling me toward something I didn't understand.

I closed my eyes, and for a single dizzying moment, I found myself back at the waterfall. Water thundered. Light shimmered. Something enormous shifted behind the white curtain—and the vines blazed in response.

My eyes flew open. "Nope. Absolutely not."

I marched back to the bed and flopped onto it, landing beside Odin, who stretched luxuriously and placed a paw on my stomach. The cat owned me.

"You're not helpful."

Odin purred louder. The grandfather clock ticked. The old hotel creaked. Somewhere in the pipes, hot water hissed. Everything felt normal. Comfortable. Safe. But I knew the truth, even if I couldn't say it out loud. That waterfall wasn't just water. And I no longer fit the version of myself I recognized. Whatever I'd stepped into hadn't asked permission. It had only waited.

The clock skipped a beat, then corrected itself.

My robe brushed against my ribs, and the vines pulsed again—quiet, insistent, warm as a second heartbeat.

I pressed both hands to my chest. "Stop it." My fingers pressed harder into my skin. "I'm not doing this. Not tonight."

I had survived worse than wonder, and I didn't owe the universe curiosity.

My reflection in the window stared back—a pale woman with flushed cheeks, wild hair, and eyes that didn't look quite the same as they had yesterday. Was that glow real? Or wishful thinking? Or maybe it was just madness?

A knock sounded faintly from down the hall—muffled voices, kitchen staff moving around, the bustle of preparing delicacies—pots clinking and voices rising.

Right. Dinner.

We still had a whole evening ahead of us.

I pushed myself upright and ran my fingers through my hair. The robe slid from my shoulders, and for a moment I stood in nothing but skin and steam-warmed air. The chill nipped at my thighs as I opened the closet and considered the few outfits hanging there.

The white bustier was a certainty. I slipped into it, fastening the small front hooks and adjusting the fabric until it sat properly against my skin.

The silk stockings took more patience. I rolled the first slowly over my calf, smoothing it upward inch by inch, enjoying the cool glide of silk against freshly washed skin. The second followed. By the time I clipped the garter hooks into place, my hands had stopped shaking.

Last came the velvet skirt. I stepped into it and drew the fabric over my hips, the soft weight settling into place.

My skin prickled, still too alive, too reactive—as if the air itself remembered how it had felt against Rurik's body.

"It's just adrenaline. Sex. Travelling. That's all." I said it like repetition could make it true.

The vines answered with one slow, glowing throb beneath my fingertips.

I shut my eyes and pretended I didn't feel it.

Rurik

The dining hall glowed in low gold light, candles trembling in their holders, pine and candle wax scenting the air.

At ten p.m., the doors would open for hotel guests, and kveldsmat would be served.

The room was calm because I required it. Every candle placed. Every table aligned. Every surface polished. Long ago, I learned that if the world could not be trusted, you built smaller ones and kept them in order.

Nine tapered candles bathed her in light. She wore a snow-white bustier fastened with delicate hooks, the boned fabric accentuating her curves, a red velvet skirt hugging her hips.

When she crossed one leg over the other, a narrow band of black silk flashed above her knee—stockings held in place by delicate garters hidden beneath the velvet. The detail felt deliberate. Intimate.

She pushed the last piece of sautéed salmon with the tines of a staghorn fork and placed the fork together with her knife.

She ran her fingertip along the raised rim of the handcrafted wooden plate, lifting her gaze to meet mine. "These are beautiful."

"Made them from the fallen branches of an ancient beech. A hobby." The memory stirred. I did not follow it.

She held me in thrall—the way her hair sat on top of her head, twirling into a snow-white crown interspersed with black braids—wispy strands resting carelessly on her slender nape.

"And this table. You made this, too?" She traced the fine grain of the ornately carved burled oak, an ancient piece crafted centuries ago, her glance teasing.

"Honey mead?" I lifted the carafe and refilled her glass. What else would I do while the world circled back to her?

Focusing on these many amusements helped keep me somewhat sane.

"Do you know how long it's been since I've come like that?" She lifted her glass slowly, gaze dragging over me before she drank. "Six times? Seven? I've lost count. I'm sore in places I didn't know could ache."

Her voice held laughter, but her pulse beat wildly at her throat.

I did not answer immediately. I imagined her beneath me—spread across linen instead of velvet, gasping my name instead of teasing me with it.

Her eyes flashed, looking at me over the rim of her glass. My first instinct was to pull her closer. I ignored it. Taking her beyond the falls had been a risk. Her essence blazed there—and whatever slept beneath the mountain noticed. The memory prowled under my skin, snapping at my control.

"Is this a family recipe? I've never tasted anything like it."

She swirled the golden elixir, watching me over the rim.

"It is." I gazed into her lovely eyes. Everything she did unsettled me—her smile, those hungry eyes.

"Look at you." Her fingers settled on my forearm. "Living your best poofy shirt life. So 'pirate'. From another era, perhaps? Medieval? Renaissance? This is linen. Don't tell me you iron your clothes, too?" She rubbed the hand-sewn hem between her fingers, a grin lifting her pouty lips.

"Would you like another helping of salmon? More Finnbiff, or perhaps a potato?" I envisioned her sinewy legs pressed against both sides of my face while I brought her to climax.

"How about we parlay back in my suite? Rustle up those sheets and see if you're good for me. Remember your promise?" She pulled her shoulders back, pushing her breasts to the forefront of the boned bustier. The velvet hem of her skirt just kissed her upper thighs. *God Jul.*

"A fine mead should never be wasted. Drink up, my lovely." I refilled both pewter goblets to the brim, unable to ignore my swelling erection. I restrained the need, not the desire.

"You enjoy teasing me, don't you? You do it on purpose." She sipped her drink before placing the goblet on the table. "Those rooms wouldn't, by any chance, be your rooms? I found a book about building Viking ships on the floor—leather with gilded illustrations. Is it yours?"

"And how old do you think I am?" The question came easily.

I watched her mouth instead of her eyes, twirling the ebony wisp between my fingers, waiting for something beneath the banter.

"Older than you look. You're far too patient for a young man," she studied me with shadowed eyes, tapping her fingernails on the pedestal of the crystal glass—rum-pa-pum-pum, in tune with piped-in festive music.

"I had a vision of you and me in the waterfall. It was otherworldly. What's the deal, Viking boy? What do you know that I don't?"

"The evening has barely begun." My thumb traced the underside of her jaw. "And I am in no hurry."

I was always in a hurry. Just not for what she thought.

"How can I make you happy?" I lifted my hand, gently

brushing the soft skin under her jaw. I resisted the urge to kiss her. The thought of her riding me—of binding herself to me before she understood—nearly broke my resolve. I could try to explain. I could show her proof of her many lives. She would not believe me. I would not risk losing her. Not now.. "What do you like?" My thumb lingered at her pulse. "Tell me."

"I think you've said that before. Hmm, what would I like? How about we paddle the pink canoe into never-never land and stay a while?" She rested her elbows on the table and propped her chin on her hand. Beneath the table, her foot brushed mine, then slid along the inside of my calf. Silk caught lightly against denim as she moved higher, the glide deliberate, unhurried. The contact was light. The message was not.

I stilled, feeling the heat of her through denim and skin, feeling the way my body reacted before my mind approved.

I closed my hand around her ankle—not to stop her, but to steady myself. The silk was smooth beneath my palm, the faint line of the garter strap pressing into my knuckles. Oh, what that woman could do with her foot.

"Tiinná has almost persuaded me to stay in Røros. There's an opening for a veterinarian." Her voice lifted into a lilt as she teased my erection with the tip of her toe.

"Perhaps I can give you a better reason?" My cock hardened as I explored her calf, sweeping my palm slowly over the silk-clad curve of her calf, feeling the heat beneath the fabric and the subtle flex of muscle as she pressed closer. My heart throbbed as I looked at her—her lower lip ready for sucking, her upper lip shaped like a bow.

"That feels amazing." Her eyes half-closed, and she

stilled, her sigh inviting exploration. I lifted her chin with my free hand, leaned in and nibbled the corner of her mouth.

When she kissed me back, I tasted her. The drums in my head grew louder. Her hands brushed through my hair as her tongue met mine. She suckled and purred.

When she paused for breath, she smiled. "You stalk my dreams. Please don't deny it. Is there something in this mead of yours? Or have you cast a spell over me?" She slid away from me, rising from her chair, her palms flat on the table, her cleavage spilling out of the tightly fitted bustier, and closed the gap between us. The velvet skirt shifted with her movement, revealing the clean line of stocking against her thigh before settling back into place.

She gently bit my bottom lip with her pretty little teeth and then traced the seam of my lips with the tip of her tongue.

I opened my eyes to see her gaze locked on mine.

"I want you, Rurik." Her hand slid over mine.

The teasing was gone. I felt the shift in her before she spoke. And another—a slow, subterranean attention turning in our direction. Not urgent—simply aware. I took her hand anyway.

"I know."

And meant far more than she could hear. The truth sat heavily in my chest. Want was the smallest part of it. What stirred beneath us already knew her. That was the danger.

"The pub can wait, ja?" I cast a furtive gaze over the empty tables. At any moment, the staff could walk in. Everything about her made my head spin.

The chair scraped the floor as I stood. My thigh caught the edge of the table—and the goblets tipped, slow at first, then all at once. The sound of shattering crystal carried too far.

"Oh, no." Her hand flew to her mouth as the glasses shattered.

The woman I longed for stood before me—her lips flushed from our last kiss.

The clean-up could wait.

Her eyes flicked to the broken glass, then back to me—bright, reckless, unafraid.

That look undid me more than the kiss had. She had no sense yet of how thin the world had become.

I took her hands and gently led her away, steering clear of the dining hall through the back service entrance and along the long corridor. I had learned long ago that if the world could not be trusted, you built smaller ones and kept them in order.

19

BONE AND VELVET

R*urik*

Holiday music played softly, mingling with voices and the clatter of silverware.

"I can't wait. I want you, Rurik." She caged me against the wall, colliding with a wreath swathed in a red bow, marking the supply closet.

Her body radiated urgency as she crushed my lips, exploring the inside of my mouth.

Thunder roared, and the walls trembled. Or was it my own heart? No forge had ever tested my restraint the way she did.

I fumbled for the door, backing us into darkness. The door shut with a muted thud, sealing in dust and the scent of pine oil. For a moment, neither of us moved. Her breath was louder in the dark. So was mine.

"Tell me to stop." My mouth hovered at hers, breath mingling, hands braced on the wall behind her.

Her laugh brushed my lips, wicked and warm. "You

first." Her fingers curled into my shirt and dragged me closer instead.

A broom toppled first, then a mop, clattering loudly against the stone floor.

She laughed against my mouth—soft, breathless, delighted—and the sound nearly broke my resolve. I stilled her with my hands on her hips. Just for a beat. Enough to feel her breathing. Enough to feel the way the air itself seemed to pause.

The ceiling fan whirred overhead. Too loud. Too fast.

I lifted her off her feet, sinking my fingers into the soft velvet covering her hips, and set her bottom on the counter.

She deepened the kiss, pulling me close, her excitement mine.

I did not touch her right away. I let the tension between us gather and press close.

Her breasts rose and fell beneath the structured white fabric, each breath brushing against my chest. I held her without moving, letting her feel exactly how hard I was through the linen of my shirt.

My body knew exactly how to take her.

My memory knew what it cost.

I could trace her blind now—the slope of her hips, the way her breath caught when I hovered but did not give. I knew the rhythm that would undo her in seconds. I also knew the rhythm that would bind her in ways she did not yet understand. My hands flexed at her waist, not from uncertainty, but from restraint tight enough to hurt.

Her gaze shifted first—heat sharpening into something heavier, something that asked and dared at the same time. Her breathing slowed instead of quickening, as if she sensed that I was holding something back and wanted to pry it loose.

Desire pressed at me from every direction—her scent, the softness of velvet beneath my palms. It would have been easy to take what she offered. To bury myself inside her and let the world narrow to heat and movement.

Instead, I slowed.

I slid my fingers beneath the edge of her bustier and flattened my palm against the heat of her skin beneath it. Not exploring. Just feeling the steady rhythm beneath my palm.

"You're shaking." Her palm flattened against my chest, feeling it.

I caught her wrist and pressed it harder against my sternum. "So are you."

Her mouth curved. The flutter at her throat betrayed her. "That's not the same thing." Her thumb traced the edge of my collarbone, testing me.

"May I?" My thumb hooked lightly beneath the edge of her bustier while my mouth traced the line of her cheek to her throat. I didn't wait for words. I waited for her breath.

It hitched.

That was answer enough.

She responded as I knew she would. A hot quiver. A low moan. Her lips parted—her heated breath at one with her hungry heart. A faint tremor rolled beneath my knees, too controlled to be footsteps.

The ink along my skin prickled, a low current moving beneath it.

"Why don't you find out?" Her glossy hair reflected a silver light. Her husky voice slid under my skin, like warm hands.

Desire hit me hard enough to blur the edges of the room. I wanted to take her exactly as she stood—lift her higher, push inside her in one hard thrust, let her cry out and not care who heard. The urge was older than thought. I closed my eyes briefly, forcing it back, reminding myself that hunger and timing were not the same thing.

I traced the boning first, following the structure that held her together. One fingertip. Then another. The sound was small but sharp in the dark. Deliberate. Intimate. Unfastening. Not stripping. I paused between each one.

After the third clasp, she stilled.

She watched my hands then, not my face. Realized I was unfastening her inch by inch, not tearing at her in desperation. Her fingers weaved through my hair, not to hurry me, but to anchor herself.

I let her breathing slow. I let myself remember why restraint mattered. When the fabric finally loosened, I didn't pull it away. I rested my forehead against hers, feeling the heat of her skin through linen and bone.

I did not remove the fabric. I let it hang open, framing her instead of revealing her. My palms slid down the outside of her thighs, velvet rasping softly under my hands. Her knees parted on their own.

The movement was unconscious. She trusted me without thinking. Trusted me not to harm what she did not yet know she was offering.

I stepped closer. Close enough that she could feel exactly where I was hard for her.

Her breath hitched.

Mine did not.

I dragged my knuckles lightly up the inside of her

thigh and stopped just shy of where she wanted me most. The muscles there flexed beneath my touch.

"Rurik," she whispered, but it wasn't a question.

I brushed my mouth along her jaw instead of answering, down the column of her throat, pausing at the hollow that fluttered with her pulse. I let my teeth graze her skin —just enough to promise more.

Still, I did not touch her where she ached.

Her fingers slid into my hair and tightened.

"You're doing this on purpose."

"Yes."

I pressed my thigh between hers, the silk of her stockings catching lightly against the linen of my trousers, friction slow. She rocked once against me, instinctively. I steadied her hips with both hands, controlling the rhythm, refusing to let her rush it.

Her lips parted.

"Don't make me beg."

I stilled.

"You think this is teasing," I whispered, my mouth brushing the corner of hers, my voice rougher than I intended. "It isn't."

Her expression shifted. Not fear. Awareness.

"Then what is it?"

I hesitated, and that hesitation alone shifted the air between us. Her expression softened, curiosity threading through the hunger.

"It's me trying not to break something." My thumb traced the inside of her wrist before I lifted her arms higher against the stone wall.

My hand finally moved where it had been denied. I slid

between her thighs, not entering, not circling—just resting my palm there. Warm. Slick. Ready.

Her body arched instantly.

I let my fingers press slightly, feeling the way she opened for me without being told. My thumb traced a line upward—barely there—just enough to draw a gasp from her mouth.

"You feel that?" I murmured.

Her nails bit into my shoulders.

"Yes."

I withdrew my hand.

She made a frustrated sound, low in her throat, and pulled me forward, trying to take what I would not yet give.

I caught her wrists gently and pinned them above her head against the cool stone wall. Not cruel. Just controlled.

Her chest rose sharply. Her eyes darkened.

"I want you inside me."

The words landed low in my body—and somewhere far older.

My jaw tightened hard enough to ache. I closed my eyes for half a heartbeat.

Snow instead of velvet. Blood instead of wine. A different sky and the same plea.

I stepped forward until my body aligned with hers, until she could feel the full length of my arousal pressed against the seam of her skirt.

Still clothed.

Still waiting.

"I know." I pressed my lips to the crown of her head. And I did nothing.

The stone under my boots shifted—not enough to shake, just enough that my balance corrected without permission. As if something had tilted its head and taken interest.

Her eyes flicked downward.

"You felt that."

"Yes."

I did not move away.

I slid my hand back down between us and finally eased two fingers inside her slowly, carefully, watching her face instead of the place where we joined.

I entered her slowly, feeling her body resist for half a breath, then soften and draw me deeper. Her head tipped back against the stone, throat exposed, breath unravelling in uneven pulls.

I worked further inside her, slow and deliberate, curling my fingers once, then again, finding the place that made her spine arch. Her hips jerked forward in response, chasing the motion.

I steadied her with my free hand at her waist.

"No," I breathed against her mouth when she tried to set the pace. "Let me."

Her lashes fluttered. Her fingers dug into my shoulders as I withdrew almost entirely—then slid back in, slower this time, fuller.

Her breath broke.

My thumb found her clitoris and traced a circle. Again. Firmer.

Her thighs quivered, anticipation building. I pressed my knee between hers, parting them.

"That's it," I murmured into her hair as I curved my fingers upward again, pressing, holding, then releasing just enough to keep her teetering on the edge.

Her hips rocked helplessly now.

"Rurik… " Her voice fractured.

I changed the rhythm. Slower. Deeper. My thumb stroking in time with the tightening inside her. Each pull coaxed another broken sound from her throat.

She wasn't playful anymore. She was coming apart.

Her head fell forward against my shoulder, breath hot against my skin as her body began to tense in that familiar, inevitable way.

"Look at me."

I caught her chin and lifted her face. Her eyes were glazed now, pupils blown wide, lips parted and trembling.

I bent my fingers once more, pressing upward with purpose.

Her back arched sharply, a cry tearing from her as her body seized around my fingers. She jolted against my hand, heels scraping the stone, her breath coming in sharp, uneven pulls. She shook against my hand, thighs trembling, breath breaking apart into helpless gasps.

I did not stop.

I kept the rhythm measured and unbroken until her knees weakened and she sagged into me.

Her breath left her in a broken exhale.

The tremor stopped the moment she did.

The corridor beyond the closet remained quiet. The music drifted faintly through the walls as if nothing in this building had changed.

I bent my head and kissed her anyway.

I eased my fingers out slowly, feeling her try to follow, hips shifting instinctively after my hand.

Her eyes snapped open, fierce and stunned. "Rurik."

Her nails dragged down my shoulders, not in anger—in demand.

I kissed her—deep, possessive, stealing the breath from her mouth while denying her the rhythm she truly wanted.

"You will have me." My mouth moved against hers, lips grazing, teeth catching lightly at her lower lip. My hand flattened against her hip to steady myself. "But not where something else can taste it."

I felt her confusion flicker beneath the heat, but I didn't let her chase it. I brushed my thumb along her lower lip, softening the bite I had left there, then rested my forehead against hers.

Her breath was still uneven. Mine was worse.

"Rurik..." Her voice had lost its edge. It was no longer a demand. It was a question she didn't know how to ask.

I smoothed the velvet of her skirt back into place, slow, deliberate. Fastened the hooks I had opened with the same care I had taken unfastening them. My knuckles brushed her ribs as I closed the last clasp. The rhythm beneath my knuckles stuttered.

"We are not hiding from the world tonight," I murmured against her temple. "We are walking into it."

I kissed her again, slower this time, my hand cupping the back of her neck.

The stone beneath us had gone still. Too still. As if whatever had shifted below had settled again—listening.

The music beyond the wall had not faltered. Laughter carried faintly down the corridor. Silverware clinked. The world continued as though nothing had shifted beneath its feet.

But it had.

I took her hand.

"Come. The market is waiting."

20

WINTER MARKET OF ECHOES

R*urik*

Under a sky twinkling with sharp, silver stars, I pushed off, sending the kicksled gliding along the snow-packed street of the Røros Christmas Market. Winter had arrived in its truest form—cold enough to bite bone.

It was no coincidence. Nothing like this ever was when she returned.

Cristabel was the catalyst.

The land felt her before the people did. Stone first—hands pressed to it, blood spilled against it, her name breaking in other mouths. It held the weight of bodies—prayer, fear—endings the living called beginnings. Heat where no fire burned. Cold where blood once cooled too fast.

The frost witches sensed it first, huddling in groups near the market stalls, their braids snapping in the wind. The huldrefolk drifted from the tree line—shadows with eyes too bright, scanning the humans through fir boughs heavy with snow. Even the elves abandoned subtlety, their gazes tracking every shimmer in the air—not looking at her directly, never that, but orienting around her all the same.

The humans didn't feel the shift. They never did. They dressed warmer, whispering about record lows on the nightly news.

The ancients knew better.

They knew what had been buried. Buried did not mean gone. It meant waiting.

Magic recoiled when her flame returned—the instinct to step back from her light.

The sled glided onward, passing frosted windowpanes and flickering ice candles, their light bending strangely—not bowing, exactly, but adjusting—as if recalibrating around a returned source.

"Stop! Don't go so fast!" She regained her grip on the kick-sled, shrieking, then laughing.

"Hold tight." I leaned into it, gliding toward the glittering lights.

"This is so much fun." She lifted her face, looking more than adorable in her winter wear—her puffy pink coat and winter leggings.

Her laughter cut clean and bright through the night—too bright. Joy was not quiet. It carried.

"Here we are." I slid to a stop in front of one particular market stall and offered Cristabel my hand.

"Where are we? I don't see a pub." She rose to her feet and tossed her heavy mane, throwing snowflakes in all directions.

A trader busy with holiday shoppers stood behind a rustic wooden stall, garlands sparkling from the canvas-covered roof. He displayed a fine selection of fur hats, deerskin mitts, woollen socks, and hand-knit sweaters on tables and tiered shelves, but I couldn't divert my gaze from the provocative pout of her lips.

"You need a hat." I touched the glistening strand of ebony. My mind replayed the hour before. I forced it down.

"A hat?" Her eyes shimmered, her lips curving into a smile, as if she were reading my mind.

"Hmm, your hair is wet." I worried she would catch a chill.

"You know how to impress. I'll give you that. Ten orgasms, not that I'm counting—and now a hat?" She pressed her index fingers to my lips.

"Not just any hat." I walked with her to the other side of the trader's booth, zeroing in on a brilliant blue woollen hat with a pompom dangling from the pointed end. "How about this one?"

"Too long. I'll look like a gnome or maybe a troll. Oh, look. Here's a pink one." She sorted through the stand-up display, choosing a knit cap with a flowing tassel. "What do you think? Pink on pink? Is it too much?"

"It's perfect, like you." I meant it more carefully than she knew. I kissed her forehead, loose strands of wool tickling my face. I paid the trader, but when I turned, she was nowhere to be found.

A cold prickle slipped down my spine—an instinct older than this town, older than my mortal disguise.

She had been right beside me, yet for one heartbeat I couldn't sense her at all. The world did not lose her—it folded around the space she should have occupied, like breath held too long. I had felt that pause before—the world forgetting how to hold her.

In other lives, it ended in silence.

My heart wrenched as I scanned the streetscape, bobbing heads passing one another, voices beckoning—Norwegian, English—some in the old language. Merry Christmas. *God Jul.*

"Look what I found. How decadent is this?"

Relief was dangerous. It softened vigilance. Vigilance was the only reason she stood beside me.

The shadows beneath the market stalls didn't move—but something inside them watched. The old hunger woke where it slept. Drawn to her, like always.

The deep places stirred.

Mine. The word did not leave my mouth. It came from below.

My pulse skipped.

The whisper brushed the edge of my senses, a ghost of a voice I had prayed never to hear again.

Snow crunched underfoot as her arm brushed mine. She handed me a waffle on a stick, while biting down on the tip of her own—a Christmas tree dipped in chocolate.

"This is fabulous. Oh my God, you have it here, too? Food delivery? What's it called? 'Dashing through the Snow?'" She pointed to a boy, head-to-toe in waterproof gear, riding a fat-tired bike. He wore a red helmet, a safety vest emblazoned with reflective tape, and an oversized, insulated backpack strapped over his shoulders.

"Do you want to go for a walk, or should we take the kick-sled?" I hooked my arm around her elbow.

"You can slide my kick-sled anytime, big boy." Her grin set my heart on fire.

"Your chariot awaits, my angel." I led her away from the crowds.

"Okay, you need to stop this. Let's walk. I love this town. It's so Christmassy." She looked up at the icicles hanging from the eaves of steeply pitched roofs, reflecting the twinkling lights.

For the first time in years, I allowed myself to see what others must see.

"What? What's wrong?" She grabbed my hand.

"You look good." My gaze refused to leave her beautiful face. I had missed her so much.

"I look good. That's all you got?" She pinched her lips together, her golden eyes reflecting heat.

"You are the fairest of them all." I kissed the tip of her turned-up nose. "Pink suits you."

"You're making me blush." She wrapped her arms around my waist and, lifting her face, pressed a firm kiss on my lips.

In the gaps between buildings, dark vents breathed warm air from the mines below—slow, measured exhales that did not belong to any furnace or pipe.

The mines had been carved by human hands—but only where the mountain allowed. The stone remembered how to breathe long before humans taught it how to burn.

Cristabel didn't notice them.

The warmth rose and fell in a rhythm I knew too well.

Not hunger. Attention.

My foot slid half a step forward before I caught myself—a reflex, sharp and immediate, the urge to place myself between her and whatever stirred below. I forced stillness into my bones, willing the reaction back into silence. Not yet. Not in front of her.

It had turned toward her—not for permission, but for proof. And now it knew where to find her.

I had failed her once by mistaking patience for mercy. I would not do so again.

The market lights flickered once—not enough for humans to notice. Enough for me.

The world had marked her again, and watching would not be enough. It would want her closer.

Snow drifted down between the rooftops, thickening the air with smoke and pine and roasting meat. Music carried from the far end of the square—fiddle and drum, laughter rising around a bonfire that burned high enough to challenge the cold.

Cristabel tugged at my hand.

"Come on. That looks like our kind of trouble."

Our kind of trouble.

If only she knew.

I let her pull me toward the fire.

The ground noticed our passing.

21

THE BONFIRE THAT KNEW MY NAME

R*urik*

"We're almost there. Just around the next corner." I glanced sideways, unable to think straight.

"Geez, look at this. Does the fun ever end? It's Santa and his reindeer." She joined the throngs of children gathered around the Santa elf—his cheeks rosy beneath his snowy beard. Behind the cedar rail fence, an eight-point buck chewed its cud, unfazed by the cooing crowd.

" 'Tis the season." I stood with my hands in my pockets, my soul whispering words of happiness.

This night had been marked long before lanterns or markets. Fires like this had been lit for her before—not for warmth, but for witnessing. I had stood at their edges in other forms, other names, knowing what came next and never stopping it in time.

"That's just so cool. We would never see this back home. Which way now?" She looked into my eyes, her face glowing with happiness.

The reindeer dipped its massive head, exhaling a plume of steam into the frozen night. Its dark eyes on *her*.

The breath lingered too long in the cold. Not submission. Knowing.

A prickle danced along my spine.

"It's so cute." Cristabel laughed, unaware.

I was not unaware. Animals near the deep places always sensed her return. I resisted the urge to sweep her away.

The ground hummed beneath the packed snow. Holding myself still took effort—control pulled tight across instincts bred for war and warding. Every step beside her required it.

Just once, my foot slipped half a pace out of rhythm—muscle memory flaring sharp, ancient, ready.

Too soon had killed her once before.

I steadied myself and kept walking.

She glanced up at me, brow faintly creased.

"You okay?"

"Fine. Crowds." I tightened my grip on her elbow, guiding her beyond the walled entrance into a long alley, weaving through standing bodies—some caught in the shadows, some drawn to the light.

"It looks like the whole town is here. Oh, look, a bonfire." She pointed to the cauldron, sending orange flames shooting into the night.

The fire cracked too deeply for pine alone. The sound wasn't sharp—it was hollow, like something opening rather than breaking.

Heat rolled up through the stones beneath our boots—like something far below had stirred and settled again.

I did not look down. Some things were answered better when ignored.

She stayed close, as if she sensed the otherness of this place, her gaze searching the crowd for her friend.

"Cristabel!" The willowy elf, her eyes flickering with magical prowess, seemed to appear out of nowhere. She was one of many living in the mortal world.

"Tiinná, there you are." Cristabel's voice rang out.

Tiinná appeared the way her kind often did—no footfall, no warning, just sudden presence. Her magic flared when she looked at Cristabel. Brighter than it should have. Worry. Something else. She knew the signs. She always had. Tiinná had intervened before—gently, disastrously, always too late. Whatever her reasons, they had never been simple.

"Hey, girl—your cheeks are glowing like a soul newly touched." Tiinná's eyes flicked to mine for the briefest moment. A warning. A question. She could sense what I sensed: Cristabel's awakening had begun.

"I'm having a wonderful time, Tiinná. This place is magical." She grinned, yet her grip on my fingers tightened. Somewhere deep inside her soul, had she remembered?

"Hey, nice hat. It's so you." The elf rested her hands on Cristabel's shoulders and kissed her cheeks, one then the other. "Drinks all around, yeah? *Juleøl*?"

"Yule-ull?" Cristabel lifted an eyebrow, glancing from her friend to me.

Tiinná laughed softly. "*Juleøl*," she corrected, rounding the word with care. "Holiday beer. Dark, spiced. Dangerous if you're not paying attention."

"Ah." Cristabel smiled, unbothered. "Yule-ull sounds friendlier."

"It isn't." Tiinná looked at me."Three mugs of *Juleøl*?"

"A definite must. Any tavern worth its salt has a holiday brew of its own, darker than regular brews. Something spicy—like you." I leaned in and whispered in her ear.

"So revved up, Rurik. I've never seen you like this. So how about it? *Juleøl, ja*?" Tiinná's smile came a half-second late. Her eyes flicked—not toward Cristabel, but toward the ground—then back again, bright and careless as ever. As if she were listening for a sound that hadn't reached the surface yet.

The fire popped sharply. Not sparks—one clean crack, like stone splitting.

Cristabel startled, her laugh cutting off as she took a half-step back. Her heel slipped on the packed snow, and she would have fallen if I hadn't caught her elbow.

"Whoa," she breathed, then laughed again, shaking it off. "Guess I got distracted."

Her pulse leapt under my fingers. Too fast. Not fear. Not surprise. Recognition without language—the most dangerous kind.

Around the cauldron, the flames leaned inward for a heartbeat—then straightened, roaring brighter than before.

No one else noticed.

But the heat underfoot did not fade.

"I'll be back." I kissed Cristabel's forehead, turning toward the tavern.

"I've got this, Rurik, don't worry." The elf slapped my arm, giving me a glowing side-eye glance.

Tiinná had kept Cristabel from me for years—a truth

we would confront one day, though not this one. This day belonged to celebration, to her victory and to mine.

Still, a part of me wished she'd remained hidden. As bitter as it was to admit, Cristabel was safer beyond my reach.

I glanced over my shoulder, finding my woman laughing among the undying. I let my senses drift through their essences, testing each for threat, unwilling to leave her safety to chance.

The fire would remember her now.

It always did.

CRISTABEL

The heat from the bonfire licked at my cheeks while snowflakes melted on my lashes, and for one breath, the whole world felt dipped in gold—lanterns swinging overhead, people laughing, the smell of pine pitch and mulled spices floating through the alley.

The fire popped sharply, louder than it should have been. A flare of sparks leapt higher than the rest—brief, unruly—before settling back into the coals.

My vines answered with a quick, startled pulse.

Rurik brushed my hand once before heading for the tavern doors. "I'll grab the *Juleøl,*" he murmured, and then he was swallowed by the crowd.

The space he'd occupied didn't close the way it should have. It stayed open—cooler somehow. The world had missed a step. The absence tugged at me harder than it should have. Something in me expected him to stay between me and whatever came next.

I tried not to stare after him like a lost puppy.

The air shifted the moment he was gone. Not colder. Not warmer. Just different. And my vines fluttered—soft as a fingertip tracing the inside of my ribs.

Tiinná's friends gathered around the bonfire, their faces glowing orange, their laughter bright enough to light the whole damn street. And yet every one of them looked at me like they knew something I didn't.

"Cristabel!" one of them called, patting the space beside her on a wooden bench.

I stepped closer, the fire warming my boots.

"You're radiant tonight," the silver-blonde woman said, her head tilted, her eyes a little too sharp. "As if the mountain air woke something in you."

Their smiles held the careful politeness of people standing too close to a ledge. Friendly—but bracing for the fall.

"Uh…thanks? The humidity, maybe," I joked, even though nothing about this place was humid. The air was knife-sharp, glittering with frost.

The women chuckled politely, but their gazes lingered. Not flirty. Not judgmental. More like I reminded them of a song they half remembered—and weren't sure they liked it.

A shift of weight sounded behind me. I turned. Nothing. Just the alley, just the bonfire, shadows stretching long from the steep roofs. Still, a prickle slid up my spine.

I had the distinct, uncomfortable sense of being found.

My vines pulsed again—hot and sudden. Wrong. I pressed my palm to my collarbone. "Oh, come on," I muttered under my breath. "Not now."

Tiinná appeared at my side with that maddening, mischievous grin.

"Feeling it, aren't you?" she whispered—just loud enough for the fire to catch her words.

I blinked. "Feeling what?"

A shiver ran up my spine. Part of me already knew the answer—I just wasn't ready to say it. But she only winked, like she'd just shared the punchline of a joke I hadn't heard. I swallowed hard, suddenly aware of the way some people were watching from across the alley—quick glances they tried to hide. One old man even bowed his head slightly before looking away.

Why did they look at me like they recognized something I didn't? Something I was supposed to remember?

"Okay," I murmured to myself, "that's not normal."

The ground beneath the wooden planks seemed to… hum. Just once. Like something shifting below.

Warm air lifted through the seams between the boards, faint but intentional—like the mountain loosening something it had kept clenched.

A breath—not mine—brushed the back of my neck.

There you are.

Not a voice. A certainty.

It wasn't a greeting. It was a claim.

I spun around, heart hammering, but no one was behind me. Just shadows stretched long from the fire. A sound rose from beneath the boards under our boots—a faint, hollow note. Too soft to be sound—too shaped to be nothing.

My boot skidded—not forward, not back. Just sideways, as if the ground decided I belonged elsewhere. I laughed it off, but the feeling stayed—like the world had shifted around me instead of the other way around.

No one else reacted—only me. My vines pulsed in answer, too warm, too alive.

Jet lag. Adrenaline. And the stupidly attractive Viking who'd made my brain short-circuit all day. Nothing supernatural. Nothing weird. Just Norway being charming and creepy at the same time.

Still, the soles of my boots felt warmer than they should have—heat lingering where the ground touched me, slow and patient.

I drew my coat tighter and looked toward the tavern doorway, where Rurik's broad silhouette finally appeared, mugs in hand.

Relief hit me so suddenly I almost laughed. Whatever that strange moment was, it evaporated the instant he looked at me. The vines quieted—alert, not calm.

Quiet wasn't relief. It was watchfulness holding its breath.

I exhaled. Everything was fine. Totally fine. I was just tired. And tipsy. And way too into a man with a ridiculous jawline.

Still… I couldn't shake the feeling that the bonfire wasn't the only thing paying attention.

~

Rurik

Snow drifted uninvited across the tavern floor. Lanterns swayed from weathered timbers, barnboards holding the dark like a secret. Beneath us, the tunnels breathed—a slow exhale from the underworld, faint as ash on wind.

She lives.

And something ancient wakes with her. Not air—intention. The mountain knew the difference, even if the mortals above did not.

My blood ran cold.

My hand twitched at my side—an instinctive reach, as if I could brace the earth itself. I forced the motion still. Touching the earth here would only remind it who I was—and who she was to it.

Some recognitions could not be undone.

A shudder rippled down my spine—not from what stood above or around us, but from what waited below, patient enough to remember.

I clenched my jaw.

Not now. Not this life.

I would not lose her again—not to fate, and not to the thing clawing its way back to the waking world.

The bartender poured jug after jug of frosty *Juleøl,* the air thick with malt and laughter. When my turn came, I tipped him, scooped up three brimming mugs, and slipped through the crush of bodies, the cold clinging to the glass like breath on a window.

A flash split the sky, and for a heartbeat, I saw Cristabel walking toward me in white. I shook my head to block out the drunken voices' loud peals.

"Tomorrow's the big day, Tiinná. Are you excited?" A size zero woman batted Tiinná's arm.

"You're throwing away your freedom, girl. So many good men out there," a round-faced female chirped.

"Lucinda, how can you say that? Lars is a pussycat.

And a passionate lover." The elf tossed her pink tongue across bowed lips, teasing the air with swirling fingertips, her laughter bubbling over.

"Where can I get myself some, girls?" A wrinkled hag joined the mix, an ancient from another time.

"Ladies, listen up. Cristabel's a veterinarian. Jordi, tell Cristabel about the studies in Oslo, the chronic wasting disease affecting the reindeer herds?" The elf nodded her head, gazing from one woman to the other.

"The zombie disease? I wrote my thesis on CWD." Cristabel fixated on the conversation, her eyes captivated.

A shiver crawled through me. Not fear—memory. CWD, the mortals called it—a brain-rotting plague. The elders had another word for it—something older than "disease"—a word that tasted like rust and ash. A word spoken only in the deep places. A hunger that learned to wear sickness. It had crawled out of the black tunnels long before anyone thought to name it.

Cristabel's interest in it was no coincidence. Her soul always circled the same dangers, the same hunger—life after life. She did not call to it. She never had. She simply existed—and the old things remembered. Like me, drawn toward her heat, dazzled. Her eyes lit up as I drew closer.

Tiinná raised her mug. "Thanks, Rurik."

Cristabel lifted hers a heartbeat later, smiling over the rim.

I drank from mine—cold, crisp, grounding. The tavern smelled of malt and pine, but she smelled like heat and memory. Standing this close to her made it harder to tell where vigilance ended and wanting began.

Wanting had ruined me before.

"Tiinná was telling me about the zombie disease

affecting reindeer herds." Cristabel's voice carried warmth that reached straight into the centuries I'd lived without her.

I bent toward her ear.

"The stars dim to your beauty."

Her grin was pure light. Pure danger. I had seen that same smile fade in other lives—always right before the world decided it could not afford her joy.

"Tiinná, I'm going to call it a night. It's nice to meet all of you." She smiled at the glowing faces and hugged the elf.

"You're leaving so soon? But the night is young." Tiinná wrapped us in a big bear hug, disappointment lingering in her voice. "No worries, I'll see you tomorrow."

As Cristabel hugged Tiinná goodbye, the lantern nearest the door guttered. A draft slid over the back of my neck—cold, damp, metallic. The flame bent sideways, guttered low, then steadied, as if something below had drawn breath and released it again.

In the forgotten shafts and buried veins of the mountain, something shifted. It did not rise. It only noticed.

"Do you want to stay? I can meet up with you later." I tugged the pom-pom on her hat.

For half a heartbeat, I nearly said her true name—the one the tunnels still whispered. I swallowed it down, hard enough that my jaw ached.

"Hey, there will be plenty of girl time later." She punched my arm.

"I hadn't planned to ruin this for you."

"You're not. And besides, Tiinná intended for this to happen." Her gaze swept through the crowd back to the smiling elf. "She told me to stay at the Gårdshuset. Said my heart would lead me here one day." She traced her fingers along my jaw. "So what now, sexy man? Snow angels? Starry ride?"

She said it—never knowing how many lives had ended on promises just like that.

My thoughts turned once, slow and sharp. Tiinná had left Norway years ago. Whatever had whispered to her—it wasn't mortal.

"I promised to please my woman," I curled my fingers around hers. "I keep my promises."

We moved through the thinning crowd toward the waiting kick sled, smoke and pine resin clinging to the air.

"Did you see that?" Her gaze caught on a huldre near the cheese stalls—its eyes too dark, too old. She blinked. "Never mind. What did you say about snow angels?" she asked as she settled into the sled, smiling—but something in her expression flickered, as if another thought had almost surfaced.

"Hold that thought." I tucked the blanket around her, kissing the top of her head.

The road dipped, and the market sounds vanished behind us like a curtain falling.

Behind us, the fire burned on.

22

WHISPERS IN THE AURORA

R*urik*

Frost-laden fields stretched into the blue night. Winter pressed against our faces. Steel slicing snow—steady, rhythmic, the only sound.

"Let's sing," Cristabel exclaimed, belting out the familiar lyrics off-key.

I joined her soprano pitch with my own rumble and heard her smile. Her voice cracked. Laughter followed.

The summit rose beneath a twisting sky threaded with ribbons of light—purple and pink bolts falling from the heavens. The sky answered her the way the stone had—not with welcome, but with attention.

"Oh my God, the sky is dancing. Where are we?" She leapt off the sled, her arms spinning like a dancing star.

"Some call it Bifrost. A bridge. A meeting of cold air and light." I caught her in mid-flight and held her in my arms.

"Okay, Viking boy, where did that come from?" Her

eyes pierced mine, then lifted into the cosmos. "Wow, the sky's on fucking steroids. Does this happen often?"

"When the temperatures drop. When the skies are clear." I wondered if the truth would chase her away. So much had happened in the last twenty-four hours.

"You promised me snow angels, handsome man. Come on, show me what you've got." She spread her arms and fell backward into the snow, sending crystals flying—her questions forgotten. She waved her arms and legs back and forth, then jumped up and examined her image embedded in the snow. "Not bad, huh?"

She was the same. Laughing at the sky as if it belonged to her.

"Your turn. Don't be a party pooper. Come on." She planted her hands on her hips, tilting her head, her rosebud lips poised to bloom.

"Okay." I dropped backward, sweeping my arms and legs, making my snow angel beside hers.

Far off in the valley, beneath the snow-packed crust of the world, a hollow boom echoed—too low for mortal ears, but it struck the ancient chord inside me.

Stone shifted far beneath us, not upward—but sideways. Learning the paths again.

Cristabel laughed beside me, making snow angels. Her breath misted in the cold.

She had no idea.

But tonight she was alive, vibrant, burning. And until the last breath, I would be the thing it reached first.

"Is that Odin? Or maybe Thor? Mine looks…like a tiny fairy." She scrunched her face, then laughed, bells ringing across the universe.

"How about a nightcap? Something to warm you?" I unscrewed the cap and offered the silver flask.

"I love this stuff. Reminds me of candy hearts—though it gives one hell of a hangover." She sniffed the contents and then swilled from the silver flask, her eyes closing. "You know, one day you'll make someone a fantabulous husband."

"Not just anyone's." I pulled her into my arms, resting my lips on the crown of her head.

"You're not giving this up, are you?" Her voice quieted, and then she lifted her chin. "You are the most interesting man in the room, I'll give you that, Rurik Andersen."

"And you are a goddess meant to be adored."

"Well, all righty, then. Should I call my mother?" Under the swirling Norwegian sky, her eyes caught the light—violet for a heartbeat.

"Was that a yes?" I cupped her face in my hands, starstruck.

"Before you go tangling your tongue with mine, let me drop a little truth bomb on you. "These—well, these beauties are artificial, mass-produced sacs of saline." She flattened her hands over them, not joking now. "Gut check time, Rurik. I survived the big C. I don't get guarantees. Tomorrow is… optional. Are you ready for that?"

She pulled no punches. Her blunt honesty turned my world upside down.

"As long as forever." The words left me before I could temper them. I dropped to one knee without thinking.

Cristabel blinked.

The laughter slipped first. Then the colour from her lips.

"You don't get to promise forever like that."

A beat.

"Not to someone who just told you tomorrow isn't guaranteed."

But she didn't step back.

A hand around her throat—neither human nor merciful.

Her body slack in my arms.

Her final breath shaping a name that wasn't mine.

I forced the memory down. Not here. Not now.

"Why do I feel I've known you forever? What is this between us?" She bared her slender fingers, tracing the outline of my jaw. "Rise, my honourable knight!"

"May I kiss you?" I took her hands in mine. Did she know who we were to one another? Did she see?

She searched my face—not for destiny, not for answers—just for truth she could feel.

"Yes, but don't make it mean more than this moment."

I kissed her like I meant to stay.

Not gentle. Not desperate. There, in the moment.

Her breath caught. Mine followed.

For one impossible heartbeat, nothing else existed. The sky burned bright and indifferent. The mountain stilled.

Loving her would cost me what little I had left.

~

Cristabel

The emerald lights tore across the sky. I forgot to breathe. Had I agreed to marry him? I thought I had.

Talk about reckless timing.

What realm had I dropped into?

"How about another swig of that panty-remover? Is that 40 proof?"

"When a warrior dies in battle, the Valkyries lead their spirit bodies across Bifrost to live in Odin's shining hall. It is the Valkyries who choose when a warrior dies."

"How gruesome." I drained the bottle of Cinnamon Joy.

"It is an honour to be chosen. To defend Odin. To die a warrior's death." His voice rolled over me, and thunder shook the ground.

"Another myth, Rurik? Asgard? Valhalla? Valkyries? Dancing fairies with bows and arrows?" A strange certainty settled in my bones. I'd stood under this exact sky before, in another body with another name, and made the same dumb joke to the same impossible man.

Astrid. Sólveig. Edda.

The names weren't thoughts. They were echoes.

My knees softened—just slightly—as if the world had tilted.

I laughed too fast, too loud, covering the sudden need to steady myself.

The names braided together, then unravelled. I shook it off. "I blame you, and the panty-remover."

"Tales told by the skalds centuries ago." He nodded his head, a smile quirking his luscious lips.

"Fairy tales." I resisted the urge to kiss him, to throw him into the nearest snowbank and have my way with him.

A flicker burned behind my eyes—too quick to grasp.

Not a vision. A fracture.

Snow falling in a cavern lit by blue fire.

A man beyond stone bars, silver eyes burning.

Heat sparked along my wrist.

The vines inked there pulled tight against my skin—not light, not fire. Urgent. Unfinished.

I sucked in a sharp breath.

The world snapped back. Snowflakes, Rurik, the biting cold—all perfectly normal.

His hand tightened at my back. I didn't pull away.

My breath matched his without thinking.

"What is truth if not a story repeated until it hardens?" He enticed me with a long sweep of his eyelashes and a knowing glance.

"Myth and legend made for television. Or maybe a crooked politician. Let's talk about these impending nuptials. We haven't even gone all the way yet. Huh? What happened to if I pleased you, we could think about a more serious relationship? Your words, big boy. That puts us back to wait and see." I tossed my head, gazing past him, my confidence faltering.

"Ah, but I made you laugh, remember? The deal is struck." His dimples defined his cheeks, making him more kissable, more fuckable.

"Huh…you're quite the trickster. Are you sure they don't call you Loki?" Shadows grew long, cloaking him in silver shades. I planted my feet firmly beneath me.

"And what do you know about Loki?" His blue eye twinkled.

Dear God, I was lost.

"I read more than romance. I know my Norse mythology."

"You know more than you realize." His eyes softened, and I wondered where this conversation was going.

I needed something solid. Immediate. Human.

"Okay. Well, I'm calling a time-out. It's showtime, Rurik. Put your money where your mouth is. You pleased me once. Can you do it twice?" I copped a feel, dropping my palm to the apex of his denim jeans.

"Soon, our union will be complete. I promise." He searched the sky, and then his gaze returned.

The lights thinned. The sky emptied. The moon hung alone in a vast, empty sky. Black spires touched the heavens, making the impossible seem possible.

"Our union?" The words settled low before I spoke them. "You say the funniest things. Explain the spa. The waterfall. How did we get to the cabin this afternoon? Everything's fuzzy. And why am I having strange visions?" A shiver ran through me. Even my vines—my tattooed vines—felt… different. A low note humming under my skin. "And why does my body feel like it's remembering something I can't?" I closed my eyes, reliving all of it, again.

"Everything comes in its order." He placed his hand on the small of my back, guiding me toward the sled.

"Shout-out to the gods!" I waved my hand in the air. "Who are you? Chef extraordinaire? Builder of trucks? Turner of wood into fancy plates? You're making me crazy."

"Is anyone who they seem?" He turned toward me, his eyes—those strange, beautiful eyes searching mine, his words sincere and serious.

"What does that mean?" I pouted like a little girl, the cinnamon apéritif making my head spin. Or was it him and only him?

"There is a place deeper within the forest. Let me show you." He lifted my hand, kissing my bare knuckles.

"Deeper into the forest? Shit fuck. Don't you want to go back to the hotel? Hit me with that magic tongue of yours? When do I get to jump your bones? Now there's the magic question, don't you think?" I slid my sleeve across my nose and grinned, today's events flashing before me—the spa, the orgasmic bliss, the northern lights. I didn't want our time to end.

"Do you trust me?" His heated gaze made my heart clench.

"Yes." My quick answer surprised me, and maybe even him.

The word settled. Heavier than fear.

"What is this inhospitable mountain range? This primordial forest? Where are you taking me, Rurik? The land of the giants? Are angry trolls hiding behind these mountains of rock?" I smiled as Rurik circled the sled, tucking the reindeer rug over my shoulders and around my legs.

He kicked off, sending the sled through birch and spruce beneath a canopy of stars. The runners hummed.

"Utgard is the land you speak of. And beyond the otherworld lies an endless ocean where Thor's most hated enemy dwells." His voice teased my mind with memories I couldn't grasp: peat smoke and firelight, the old one speaking softly, wind rattling the roof.

"You really need to stop saying things like that." I hugged myself—but my laugh wobbled. "I don't do destiny. I barely do brunch."

My heart fluttered. Snow and ice thinned. Moss rose where winter had been. Towering erratics stood like something left behind.

"Rurik? Where are we going?" I burrowed deeper into the fur rug.

"You will see." He followed the sheltered bank of a babbling brook, moonbeams sparkling like diamonds in the sky.

I watched, unblinking, as the sled slowed. Beyond the vast green lands, a violet haze folded over the rolling fields. Reaching high into the sky, the branches of a great tree. A squirrel scurried from branch to branch. A wolf howled.

Farm buildings formed an enclosure around the giant oak. My gaze drifted from the barn to the drive shed to the lean-to stacked to the rafters with chopped cordwood, resting on the long-handled axe driven into a stump. Where had I seen that before? It hurt my head to think.

The log cabin stood alone, its sod roof tufted with frost-silvered grass, a living thing breathing in the cold. It was magical.

Something in my chest leaned toward it. But Rurik was watching. I looked into his eyes, at his furrowed brow. This homestead was someone's home.

The word *ours* moved through me without asking permission—not a thought, not a hope.

Homes were built. Bought. Lived in. They did not look at you and decide.

"Where are we? Who lives here?"

"This is our home."

For half a breath, I couldn't tell if he meant someday—or before.

"You're getting way ahead of yourself, Viking boy."

The words came easy. The feeling did not.

He offered his hand, helped me to my feet, and, without hesitation, wrapped his arms around me, tucked my face beneath his chin, and held me as if he would never let go.

23

AWAKEN, LITTLE STAR

C*ristabel*

"Our home?" Heat rolled through me, threaded with the balsam scent of him.

Rurik turned and guided me toward the cabin.

My gaze moved to the square windows, casting light across the wide planks of a covered porch, at the wreath of leathered leaves on the arched doorway—hand-hewn, carved in delicate scrolls.

My body had already decided where it belonged. You could argue with memory. This wasn't that.

"There are things I need to tell you." Rurik kicked the snow off his boots and released the forged lever.

Odin greeted us by rolling onto his back and stretching his long body on a handwoven rug, screeching his welcome.

"Would you like to sit?" He took my coat, hung it on a wrought-iron hook, and motioned toward an alcove—a wooden bench built into the wall.

I slipped off my boots, one at a time, then looked at Rurik, my fingers gripping the bench.

Red knitted booties sat by the door.

For me?

My chest tightened—not with warmth, but with the sense I'd walked into a story already in motion.

I told myself it was a coincidence. Small towns loved gestures. I needed it to be that simple.

"How did Odin get here?" I dropped to my knees and scratched the cat's tufted ears. I had questions, so many questions.

"He goes where he wants." The firelight caught in his skin. He didn't look away. "You owe me a kiss."

"What?" Who was this man standing before me? Why did I yearn for his touch? Why did my heart race in his presence?

"Look up." His face lifted toward a wide fir beam, and a prolific bundle of twigs, a globe of green leaves bursting with waxy white berries.

I caught his shirt and kissed him first.

His thumb brushed my jaw.

"I've waited for this."

"For a kiss under the mistletoe?"

His mouth curved faintly. "For you to walk back through that door."

His hand stayed at my jaw a second too long before he let it fall.

I caught his wrist before he could pull away.

"Walk back?"

The word scraped on the way out.

"You make it sound like I left."

A flicker moved through his eyes—not guilt. Not

surprise. Something older. Something that had survived the answer before I even asked it.

"You did." His tone stayed even, but his fingers flexed at his sides. "Just not the way you think."

I dropped his wrist and took a step back, my shoulder hitting the corner of the wall. The cabin felt smaller. Closer.

"How many times have I been here?"

His jaw tightened, just once. "Enough."

"That's not an answer." My laugh came out thin. "It sounds more like a countdown."

"It's the only one I can give you right now."

Right now.

I crossed my arms over my chest, buying space between us. "So that's it? I've lived here before. I've left before. And you just… wait?"

His throat moved.

"I stay."

The words hit harder than they should have.

He stepped back before I could push further, and I hated that part of me was relieved. As if too much truth would undo this fragile thing between us.

Everything about this place pressed at something just out of reach. *Our home?* I gazed from the overstuffed sofa to the bookshelf leaning against the wall. I crossed the floor, the worn planks stretching before me glowing with a soft, golden hue, drawn to the fireplace and the smooth, round stones rising into the rafters. The mantel—the hammered fasteners, the scene carved into sea-washed timber—pulled at something I couldn't name. I ran my hand over the dragon ship sailing into the harbour of a village, and a woman, her arms outstretched—a memorial from another time? The feeling came first. Grief, without a source.

My throat closed, thick with smoke that wasn't there. I stepped back from the hearth without knowing why. Too much of it felt familiar in a way I didn't want to examine.

He moved around the room, lighting one candle after another and filling the air with the most fragrant vanilla scent. He glanced up and smiled.

What kind of man collected vanilla-scented candles—and waited to light them?

"Make yourself at home." He gestured toward the sofa, then moved behind a large sand-coloured island, opening a wine cooler the size of a refrigerator, and taking out a bottle of sparkling rosé. He placed the bottle on the island. "Would you like wine?" He looked up, then cracked the seal and popped the cork.

"Um…okay." I scratched the back of my head. "You have a Christmas tree? And presents?" I approached the living branches, adorned with red baubles, the teardrop crystals reflecting the candle's glow. I inhaled the pungent scent, a memory brushing my mind, whisper soft.

Tucked between the sprawling branches and wrapped in candy-cane-striped paper, jewelry-sized boxes sat waiting—for someone.

I couldn't shake the feeling that I'd been here before. My knees softened.

"For the years I didn't have." His fingers tightened around the stem before he handed me the glass.

"For the years you didn't have?"

My voice came out thinner than I meant it to.

He didn't look at the tree. He watched me.

"There were birthdays. Winters. Mornings, I imagined you walking down those stairs."

My stomach dropped.

I gave a small, disbelieving laugh. "You're joking."

"I don't joke about this."

The air shifted.

"You wrapped gifts for someone who wasn't here?" I set the glass down harder than necessary. "That's not romantic, Rurik. That's—"

I stopped.

"For someone who always comes back."

The certainty in his voice tightened against my ribs.

"Always?" I shook my head. "You don't get to say that like it's a fact."

His jaw tightened.

"How long?" I asked.

He didn't answer. His throat moved as if he almost did.

"That's what I thought." I folded my arms, buying space between us. "You keep saying things like I'm part of some story you've already read."

His gaze didn't waver.

"I am."

The words were soft. Not dramatic. Not triumphant.

And that scared me more.

He stood very still, watching me as if blinking might cost him.

I opened my mouth to push again—to demand something concrete, something human—but the look in his eyes stopped me. Not intensity.

Fear.

I looked away first.

"This is amazing," I muttered, gesturing vaguely at the

tree, the cabin, the candles. "The wine. The décor. Very happily ever after made-for-television Christmas movie."

Deflection. Safer ground.

I walked away, my pulse skipping, needing distance before whatever he wasn't saying swallowed the room whole.

A shadowbox hung on one wall, crafted from fine wood, a miniature replica of a log cabin, depicting a man and a woman sitting together, enjoying an evening meal, with the moon shining through mullioned windows. A cat slept on the hearth.

The woman's posture mirrored mine so closely my scalp prickled.

A row of hardcovers lined the shelf—cookbooks, woodworking manuals, and one narrow spine stamped in tarnished gold.

Runes of the Elder North: Their Origins and Portents, by Rurik Andersen.

I snorted. Of course he did.

The weight in the room closed in. I reached for something lighter.

"You wrote an actual book?" I called over my shoulder. "What are you, secretly famous, and I missed it?"

"Hardly." His laugh rolled warm and low. "Just an old project. No one reads that one anymore."

The shift in his tone made me glance back, but he'd already turned away. The book's title needled my brain, though, like a half-remembered song. I let it go. There were vanilla candles and a ridiculously handsome man to worry about, not his retired projects.

I ran my fingers over a collection of instruments: a boxwood panpipe, a flute, an elaborately carved wooden lyre, and a bronze lur—a trumpet-like instrument. Sitting on the floor, a woven basket overflowed with handheld instruments: bells, whistles, flutes, and rattles.

"Don't tell me you're a musician?" I glanced over my shoulder and saw him lounging on the sofa, his feet up on the table.

A double-strung fiddle with bone inlays and a carved lion's head at the scroll. A horsehair bow hung on a hook beside the folklore piece.

"I play." He sipped his drink.

"So, you're what? A one-person band? Is this just another hobby?" I took a slow sip of the wine, pear and citrus rose from the glass, bright and sharp. I studied him. Had he been standing here the whole time, unchanged?

He shrugged, a smile tugging his lips upward.

"Okay, show me what you've got. Sing me a song." I turned away from the musical display and sat cross-legged on a large floor pillow, with an image of Rurik and this pillow filling my mind.

"Now?" His eyes flickered, light and dark, all at the same time.

"Uh, huh, yep…right now." I curled my fingers into the tufted edging.

The sofa creaked as he rose to his towering height. He looked at me and then selected an elliptical hand drum, skinned with reindeer hide and stained with Celtic designs.

My mouth dropped open when he placed a crown of antlers on his head. A giant from another world. A god. The air bent around him, his massive body at one with the shaman's drum. Even Odin paid tribute, a soft trill rumbling in his throat, his tufted ears tweaking, one then the other as Rurik struck the drum. The first strike landed, and the air changed.

"Okay," I laughed. "Just… don't make it weird."

He struck the drum. The ground shifted, the rhythm pulling me in.

For half a second, I thought about stopping him. For the other half, I realized I wouldn't.

He sang a ballad of love and loss, a tale of giants, fire-breathing monsters, destruction, and war—the melody turbulent yet moody. Ancient words—stories told in runes. A moment returned—the waterfall, the ice cavern—portals into other worlds. Shadowed figures joined the dance—spirits from another world.

His voice melted my frostbitten soul.

The drumbeat crawled under my skin. Each strike landed in my chest, not my ears—thud, thud, thud—until I couldn't tell if it was Rurik's rhythm or my heart.

The room blurred, candlelight stretching into smears of gold. The stone hearth dissolved into a wash of shadow and colour. When I blinked, the cabin was gone.

I stood beneath a tree I knew and didn't know—its trunk wider than any house, its roots twisting into darkness, its branches threading the sky. A squirrel raced along a branch. Somewhere distant, a wolf howled. The air smelled of pine, metal, and snow.

Light pulled at my sternum.

I looked down.

The vines inked over my scars began to glow—silver and green threading beneath the skin, rising through scar and ink alike.

"Cristabel." Rurik's voice echoed as if it cam
very far away.

The drumbeat slowed, and the world tilted.

The tree shattered—emerald, violet, gold—and the cabin slammed back into place: stone hearth, candlelight, fur rug, Rurik kneeling before me, antlers still crowning his head, something raw cracking through his composure.

A tear slid down my cheek. I hadn't realized I was crying.

"Did you see it?" His voice was low. "Tell me."

"I…" My lips trembled. "There was a tree. A… huge tree. And my vines were—" I squeezed my fingers together. The glow was gone, but the warmth remained. "They were…reaching for it."

For a heartbeat, everything in him stilled.

"Old rhythms can stir memory." The words sounded like hope—and warning.

His hand hovered near me, then dropped.

I knew that tree. Not as a symbol.

As a place.

The certainty landed in my bones before my mind could argue. And that terrified me more than anything he'd said.

Something inside me had woken.

It wasn't going back to sleep.

24

THE PLACE THAT WAITED

C*ristabel*

Heat tore through me, threading muscle and bone. Not new. Returning. My vision blurred at the edges.

Rurik's hands held me. His composure didn't break. It hardened.

I tried to tell him I was fine, but the words were stuck in my throat. My heartbeat sounded wrong—too loud, too close—like it didn't belong entirely to me.

I reached for him. Or maybe the world reached for me. The room stretched wider than it should, as if it, too, had been holding its breath, waiting to see whether I would stay. Everything went soft and distant—sound dulling, the world muffled as if I were hearing it through water. Thought slipped away, leaving only sensation: warmth, pressure, a pull that would not release me.

I could have stayed where I was—unclaimed, untouched by want. The pull wasn't fear. It was easy.

And still, I turned toward him.

He was there, kneeling before me, holding my face between his hands and kissing me with those luscious lips, filling me with his taste, his mouth taking mine with a patience that felt inevitable.

The kiss didn't pull me back all at once. It came in pieces—heat and breath—giving me something to hold onto.

Want coiled low in my belly, unfamiliar in its intensity. I'd wanted before—but this resonated on a deeper level, desire answering a call I hadn't known how to hear. The ache settled deep within me.

Understanding felt like a door I wasn't ready to open. Sensation was easier. Safer. I let it carry me instead.

He lifted my wool turtleneck over my head and tossed it onto the floor. The air kissed my skin. Goosebumps rose, only to be smoothed away by the weight of his palms.

He ran his fingers over my sports bra, testing the edges. "What is this?"

His knuckles brushed the curve beneath the cotton as if confirming I was real. Sensation flickered there—uneven, electric—enough to make my breath catch.

"What do you mean? What is this? It's a sports bra." I rested my hands on his broad shoulders.

For a moment, I studied him—solid, real, unmistakably present. I needed the reminder that at least one thing in the room wasn't moving under my feet.

"You hide all this in cotton?" His fingers traced the edge of the band, testing.

"Where've you been, Rurik? I speak for all women across the world when I say this—comfort rules. And the only sport I want right now is between the sheets. You've got me way past hot and bothered, don't you think?" I pulled the string of his poofy shirt, sounding a lot more confident than I felt.

"Is that what I do to you?" His thumb pressed just enough to make me answer with my body.

He slid his fingers beneath the elastic band at my ribs and tugged lightly, testing the give. The cotton stretched stubbornly as he worked it upward, his palms skimming my breasts while the fabric dragged across my skin.

"Way past that, handsome man. I'm barely holding still."I lifted my arms for him, and he peeled it over my head in one deliberate motion, the knit catching briefly at my wrists before falling to the floor.

Cool air slid over the reconstructed curve of me, skin tightening instinctively, a sharp pull racing across scar and implant alike. Not the way it once had—but enough. My breath faltered beneath his stare.

His hands framed the shape of me without hesitation, his thumb brushing over the faint scar, then the swell beneath it. Something fierce flared in my chest, settling low in my belly as his expression shifted.

"You don't hide," he murmured.

My pulse stuttered.

He lowered his hands, hooking his fingers into the waistband of my leggings, pulling them down, then sliding lower and catching my panties beneath.

He didn't pause, dragging them over the curve of my hips, across muscle and bone—until the last strip of fabric slipped past my knees.

I should have felt exposed.

Instead, I felt seen.

My fingers pressed higher, feeling the rigid line of muscle sculpting his chest. His stomach flexed under my palm, heat gathering there, contained but not untouched. I liked knowing I could do that to him. Once was enough.

The fireplace flared, sparks lifting from hardwood logs as if curious. I noticed—distantly—that nothing else in the room moved at all.

Behind him, in front of the hearth, was a broad circular platform made of dark wood, elevated by a shallow step from the floor. I hadn't truly noticed it before. It seemed less like furniture and more like something set into the bones of the house.

He lowered me onto the dais like something already promised.

The wood met my back already warm. When I shifted, the curve fit the arch of my spine perfectly, the grain pressing into my shoulder blades and hips like something anticipating my shape.

The loose cotton of his shirt brushed my stomach as he leaned over me, the fabric warm from his skin. Even that soft graze made my breath hitch.

"Am I a sacrifice to the gods, Viking boy?" I tossed my hair, stretching my arms across the wide circle. I ached for him.

Orange embers lifted from the logs, rising and falling in quiet arcs.

"I've missed you."

The words carried no apology. Only history.

It made my chest ache in a way desire couldn't touch. I wanted to ask *how long*, but the answer felt too heavy to hold.

His hands moved over me, following the path inked along my skin. He traced the thin lines at my wrist where scar and ink intertwined—then followed their curve up my forearm.

His fingers flattened over my ribs, slid over my hip, and traced lower, following the dark ink as if it were a path only he could see.

He wasn't touching me to arouse me. He was reading the story written along my skin.

When his mouth replaced his fingers, it wasn't abrupt. It was a continuation. A soft press of lips where ink darkened my skin. A slow drag of warmth, curving along my waist.

The vines pulsed, a low current sliding through ink and scar

His mouth followed them downward, across my stomach, along the dip of my hip until his breath ghosted between my thighs.

I opened without being asked.

He looked up at me then, eyes dark and unguarded.

My hands slid into his hair, not guiding, not forcing, just holding him there.

His tongue touched me slowly, tracing each vine to where it ended.

The first stroke made my hips lift.

The second made my spine arch.

His hands steadied me, spreading my thighs wider against the curve of the wood. The dais answered with a low warmth beneath my back.

My heartbeat thudded hard along my wrist—a flare beneath ink and scar—and he felt it.

He moved slowly, each stroke drawing tight circles until the air between us sparked, ready to ignite.

Heat surged through me, my breath rising and falling with his rhythm.

When he slid two fingers inside me, the stretch opened me slowly, forcing a broken sound from my throat, a slow claim that sent fire racing up my spine.

"Rurik." My voice broke.

Pleasure rose slow and deep, a tide pulling tight through my center.

He lifted his mouth from my clit just enough to breathe, then returned—firmer this time—his tongue matching the steady glide of his fingers.

The vines flared into living currents of heat, my body clenching around him. Release tore through me in a rolling wave, my vision narrowing, my body locking, and then spilling open all at once.

The stone beneath the dais hummed with a low vibration.

He didn't chase his own pleasure. He watched mine crest. And when I shattered—shaking, gasping—his hand tightened around my hip.

"I am not losing you again." The words reached somewhere deep inside me.

"You're intense," I breathed. My hands were already in his hair, the words heavy on my tongue. I wanted him—too much.

He buried his face in my hair, then kissed my forehead, trailing his lips over my cheekbones, stopping at the corner of my mouth. The scruff covering his chin tickled me.

I felt suddenly exposed—not in body, but in something

deeper. Like whatever passed between us would mark more than skin.

"I love you." His hand flattened against my hip, steadying himself.

The words settled between us.

I didn't move.

"Well, you'd better. That's how fairy tales work—happily ever after, and all that?" My hand traced the muscles defining his upper arm. "If you think there's a big dowry waiting, you're wrong. It's just me and my pink truck."

His mouth stilled against my skin.

"Don't make it smaller than it is."

The words weren't sharp. They were steady.

The flames surged higher behind him, casting his face in gold and shadow. The stone beneath me answered. The air grew dense, drawn inward like a breath held too long. The crackling logs swallowed every other sound. For a heartbeat, the room closed in—the walls listening.

Rurik didn't look back. He lifted me from the dais, cradling me in his arms, then ascended one step after another along the glass staircase.

The open collar of his shirt fell against my breasts as he gathered me close, linen grazing sensitive skin with every step.

His arms were still warm around me, my body pliant and humming, but something beneath the pleasure stirred uneasily. Not regret—nothing so clean. This wasn't ascent. It was a crossing.

I pressed a kiss to his chest anyway, breathing him in, letting desire carry me forward even as a small, quiet part of me wondered what being chosen back might demand.

The air cooled as we climbed.

Below us, the fire steadied. Each step rang softly beneath us, glass chiming as if it knew the way.

I tucked my face against his chest and let the question of where dissolve.

At that moment, I chose him.

25

THE BOOK BETWEEN US

C*ristabel*

My gaze flickered over Rurik's bedroom—an expansive space lined with pine boards, dominated by a four-poster bed wrapped in indigo blue, the headboard carved with intricate runes.

One elliptical window looked out over a horizon of sparkling stars. They didn't twinkle the way stars should. They held steady, watching. Distance worked differently here. The room itself seemed to hold—waiting.

He set me on my feet gently, trailing his fingertips over my breasts, making the soft hairs on my belly rise. My legs felt untrustworthy for a second, as if they were still catching up to the rest of me.

Heat rose in my cheeks as I watched him undress—first, his shirt, then, with one hand behind his head, he slipped a white undershirt off his sculpted chest, leaving only his jeans clinging to his thick hips. I didn't move. I couldn't. Watching him felt like crossing a line. My mouth watered as he unbuckled his belt and stepped out of the dark denim. Commando. His cock hung heavy between powerful thighs.

I wasted no time. This was what I had missed—Rurik. That golden-haired man with mismatched eyes.

There were too many questions. At this point, I didn't care. I wanted the man before me. It was that simple.

I ran my fingers over his golden skin. Muscle beneath flesh—defined. His shaft—velvet smooth, deeply veined—heavy in my palm. His eyes closed as I wrapped my fingers around his length. I wanted him like that. I wanted to ride him with his legs splayed apart. No foreplay. No slow kisses.

I needed to prove this wanting was mine. If I hesitated now, it wouldn't be.

I propelled him backwards, seating him on the edge of the oversized mattress. The bed dipped beneath his weight, the runes along the headboard catching the light. They dimmed again when he stilled.

"There are condoms in the drawer." His fingers clenched the indigo quilting, a sheen of sweat forming on his brow.

I slid off the bed, toes curling into the plush carpet, and reached for the nightstand drawer. When I pulled it open, a neat box of condoms stared back at me—still sealed.

"Brand new," I muttered. The ache wasn't jealousy. It was grief. He'd waited. Long enough to believe he might never need them. "I'm not sure these will fit. Did you check the size?"

His smile went slow and wicked.

I looked down again, hoping to regain my composure, and that's when I saw it—not the condoms, not my own shaking hands, but the book half-tucked beneath the box.

A hardcover. Deep blue dust jacket. The kind of thing you'd find in the "serious mythology" section of some academic shop.

My hands stalled.

I set the condom aside and picked up the book.

Norse Mythology Explained, by Rurik Andersen,

Illustrated by Cadence Frank.

The world tilted.

"I…" My mouth dried.

I flipped it open, and my knees went weak. The illustrations were detailed and vibrant, fluid and precise. Odin on his eight-legged stallion, Sleipnir, riding through a sky split with lightning. Thor with hammer raised, storms cracking the horizon. Loki chained beneath a mountain, a serpent dripping venom toward his face.

The shadows feathered exactly the way my hand always did. My fingers tingled, itching with the phantom memory of charcoal and ink.

Recognition hit like impact.

"This is my style," I whispered. "I've drawn this Valkyrie before. This is…this is how I sketch. How…"

My fingertips brushed one illustration: a shield-maiden on a white stallion, hair pale as snow streaked with a single dark stripe.

My hair.

The room seemed to narrow around the image, breath holding, as if something waited to see whether I would say it aloud.

"I kept it from you because every time I've told you early…I've lost you," Rurik confessed. "You look at me with wonder one moment, and the next you're gone. I couldn't bear that again." His voice lowered. "I needed one night—just one—where you were mine before the world stole you back."

He didn't look ashamed. He seemed exhausted. Loss had worn grooves into him.

I didn't just recognize the art. I recognized the moment. Mud. Iron. A battlefield smelling of blood and smoke. The stallion shifting under me. It arrived whole—weight, iron, smoke, blood. A man with mismatched eyes, lifting his face to mine as I rode toward him.

My knees buckled. My vision blurred. Grief didn't belong to one lifetime.

Rurik was suddenly there, catching me before I crumpled to the floor. His hands were firm on my arms, but his expression was raw.

"You remember her." His gaze swept mine. "At least a piece."

"Cadence." The name scraped past my lips. "The illustrator. That's what the cover says. But that's—that's me, isn't it?"

He swallowed, Adam's apple bobbing.

"In another life. Another name. Another body. Still you," he whispered.

I looked from the book to him, my heart hammering.

"This was published in 1869." I stared at the date. "That's impossible." The word should have rattled me. Instead, it settled—quiet, undeniable—like a fact my body had been storing long before my mind demanded proof.

"For a mortal. Yes."

"How old are you, Rurik? Actually?"

"By your reckoning? Three hundred and sixty winters."

The number didn't frighten me the way it should have. It settled, slotting into place like a missing piece.

I let out a sound that was half laugh, half sob. A low heat throbbed beneath my ribs—my vines stirring, aware, awake. The warmth sharpened suddenly—too focused—then eased, leaving a faint afterburn beneath my ribs. It should've terrified me. Instead…it felt right. Familiar. As if some part of me had already known he wasn't mortal.

"You don't even *look* forty," I whispered. "What are you?"

He huffed a dark laugh, his fingers trailing my hip, slow and possessive. "Gods die. So will I." The air seemed to settle around him when he spoke.

A beat. A spark.

"Until then." His lips brushed my throat, "I'm stuck in this realm, in this body…" His hand tightened on my waist. "And very, very mortal where it counts."

"How many times have I died?"

The question wasn't panic. It was inventory. It was grief without a grave. I forced a laugh I didn't feel.

His eyes closed for a heartbeat.

"Enough that I stopped counting. You return. You always return. With a new name—a new life. I find you. I lose you. I try again."

I looked down at the book, at Cadence's signature looping along the bottom of a Valkyrie's cloak.

"And you're saying I illustrated this in another life. I was Cadence Frank. I loved you then, too."

His gaze searched mine, desperate and reverent all at once.

"You found me in ink before you found me in flesh.

Even in that life, you drew what you remembered. You… didn't know why."

My chest ached. Beneath my scars, the vines warmed in a slow throb, like something waking up.

"This is insane," I whispered. "This is—" I looked up at him. "Why tell me now? Why tonight?"

He lifted the small foil square from the bedspread, turning it between his fingers.

"Because once I do this, there is no going back." His voice rumbled low.

My heart didn't race in fear. It ran like it was coming home.

"What do you mean?" My stomach flipped. "It's just sex, Rurik. I'm a vet, not a virgin."

"You are human."

His fingers tightened on my waist.

"And you are not."

He set the condom on the nightstand beside the open book.

"If I wear this, you will feel pleasure. Nothing else." He motioned toward the wrapper.

His words echoed unpleasantly, catching on something deep in my chest. This wasn't about sex. I could feel that clearly now. It was about how much of myself I was willing to reclaim in one night—and how much I was willing to risk never being able to forget again.

Heat climbed my neck.

"And without it?" My voice was a whisper.

"Without it, you wake."

His gaze held mine.

"And things change. You remember. All of it."

The word remember pressed somewhere deep in my ribs.

"A curse?" I almost laughed. It sounded medieval.

"It has killed you three times." A muscle feathered in his jaw. Something in his gaze went colder.

The words landed without drama. That made them worse.

"When I wake… does it wake too?" I asked quietly.

He didn't hesitate. "It stirs when you do."

My mouth went dry.

I wrapped my arms around myself, suddenly aware of how fragile one body could be.

"And if we don't—" I gestured between us, suddenly shy. "If we use the condom. What happens then?"

"Then you go back to the hotel. You live your life. Perhaps you will come back here one day. Perhaps not. I will watch from afar. I will wait."

"That's cruel." A hollow ache opened beneath my ribs.

"It is survival. For you."

"And for you?"

"For me, it is another lifetime of wanting." He had already survived that.

Silence stretched between us—thick with memory, heavier than desire.

My heart knew the answer long before my mouth formed the words.

"I'm a cancer survivor, Rurik." My voice was quiet and calm. "I already learned what waiting gets you." Even if I didn't fully understand what I was agreeing to.

The vines beneath my scars pulsed once, in agreement.

"Are you sure?"

"No. But I trust you." I touched his hand.

"That is enough," he whispered.

The danger in him softened—but did not disappear.

"If you fall again, I won't accept it." He went still. "I won't let it happen again."

He set the condom aside without ceremony and stepped toward me. For a heartbeat, we just stood there, our reflections caught in the dark window, aurora dancing faintly beyond. Desire still hummed between us, warm and undeniable—but beneath it stirred something quieter.

Once this was done, there would be no half-measures left.

Whatever waited felt older than the room—and far closer than it should have been.

I didn't step back.

26

THE OLD WAY

C*ristabel*

I shivered, not from cold—but from knowing. Mine. The words should have frightened me. They didn't. They settled into my bones like a memory long buried.

The certainty felt too large to hold—but I didn't reject it. It leaned in, accepting it, as if I'd carried it before.

That was the strangest part. Nothing in me disappeared to make room for him. I was still myself. Still choosing—just choosing something that would alter everything.

"I have searched the world over to find you. From this life to the next. You make eternity worth living." The bed creaked under his weight as he sat beside me, perfectly still.

This wasn't hunger. This was survival tempered into patience. The realization made my chest ache in a way desire couldn't soothe.

He didn't say the years aloud—the empty beds, the watching, the restraint. They lived in the stillness of his body, in the way he touched me like I might vanish if he moved too fast.

"And you're mine? Is that what you're saying?" Somehow, the unimaginable just landed in my lap.

"I am. I will be yours for as long as the stars shine in the sky." He placed his hand on my knee, his thumb stroking my calf.

"And you can't die? What are you? A god? Like Odin? Like Thor? Is that what you're saying?" I shook my head, knowing he spoke the truth.

"I will die when Ragnarök comes. The future is foretold." His chin lowered, his dark hair falling over his brow.

"Ragnarök." The name slid into place like something rehearsed long ago, waiting for the right mouth to say it again. I didn't *know* it. I recognized it—like a scar you forget until something brushes it just right.

"Ragnarök is when the end…" He tilted his head and met my gaze.

"I know what Ragnarök is. Jesus fucking Christ… I've been reborn? Reincarnated. How many times have I died?"

The question wasn't panic. It was accounting.

"And I fall in love with you? Every time? Is that what you're saying?" I swallowed hard.

He walked the floor, unguarded now—desire heavy and undeniable against his abdomen. The contrast—ancient truth and raw, living flesh—made my breath stutter.

He was myth and male at once.

My body ached, wanting him, needing him.

"What about pregnancy?"

I hadn't known I was carrying that grief until the question gave it shape. It wasn't the absence that hurt. It was the possibility that somewhere, in some life, I had wanted them badly enough to mourn them without ever meeting them.

"If it pleases fate." He dipped his head, kissing my forehead. "But no, we have not been blessed with children. You are a human, and I am not. It would be unlikely. If you want children, perhaps we should forget all of this. I will take you back to the hotel."

"Stop talking, Rurik. I love you. I've always loved you. I didn't know it, but it's true." I left the bed and leaned into him, wrapping myself in his warmth, my clitoris brushing his erect shaft. "What realm are you from? Is this another plane of existence?"

"Asgard, and yes, where we are right now, is the old world. The same place. Another time." He ran his fingers through my hair, his voice coursing through me. "Everything about you—every finger, every limb—meant for my lips."

"You have a wine cooler in the Old World? And vanilla-scented candles?" I closed my eyes, breathing him in. I knew what I wanted and what I needed. "No more games, Rurik. You've put me off long enough. Sit down on the bed. Please."

His breath left him, his voice hissing when I reached for him, and when I ran my fingers along his length.

"You're right about one thing, handsome man. You're mine—all mine."

I settled into his lap, feeling the warmth rolling off him

He was thick and solid, and I could feel him pulse against me before I even took him inside. My thighs trembled as I settled over him, the heavy length of him brushing the slick heat between my legs.

His hands didn't move. He gripped the bedding, knuckles whitening. He let me decide.

I gripped his shoulders as the broad head of him pressed against me, nudging, stretching me open in increments that made my breath catch. I lowered myself a fraction at a time, feeling my body accommodate him, claim him, welcome him.

It wasn't just friction. I knew this shape.

It didn't resist. It answered.

A low sound tore from his chest—not impatience, not dominance—relief. As if he had been holding himself at the edge of starvation for centuries.

"More," I whispered.

Not because he demanded it—because I did.

I sank down fully, and the stretch burned sweet and deep. His breath brushed my collarbone, warm and uneven. My hands flattened against his chest, feeling the steady thud of his heart beneath my palms—too strong to belong to an ordinary man.

Sweat gathered where our skin met.

Lightning cracked overhead.

Something low in my belly tightened in response. I moved carefully at first, each slide slow and deliberate. Every inch measured against my breath. My body clutched him, pulling him deeper.

My hips jerked forward without permission, the rhythm building, like waves cresting over the shoreline.

My heartbeat climbed into my throat, skin flushing, the air between us thickening until even breathing felt intimate.

"Cristabel." The way he said my name sounded older than language.

"You're too tight. I don't want to hurt you." His thumbs pressed into my hips, grounding me.

"More." Something split through me, tearing me into two distinct parts. The present. The past. The shadows called to me. So many voices. So many faces.

They didn't frighten me. The strange thing was how *familiar* they felt. They crowded close—faces without names, emotions without scenes—echoes pressing at a door I hadn't known existed. Love was the loudest among them—love, loss, and the unbearable relief of finding him again.

All of it converged on this moment—this body, this bed, this man—as if every version of me had been walking here all along. Not summoned. Just…arrived.

His voice shook—not with need, but with the weight of finally being allowed to want without restraint. Every lifetime before this had ended with him holding back, watching me fade, promising himself never to need this much again.

Tonight, I wasn't fading. I was choosing him. This wasn't permission—it was claiming.

"Take all of me. My sweet, sweet angel." His fingers curled, his knuckles whitening.

His cock jerked, driving inward with pulsing determination—a being with a mind of its own. The thrust knocked the breath from my lungs. I rocked harder, taking more of him, my thighs tightening as pleasure built sharp and fast beneath my skin.

I opened my eyes and found him gazing at me, his eyes glowing bright—a god of the otherworld. How had this supernatural being become mine? A question for another day. I needed only one thing. I arched into him, my hair falling over my back, and clenched my thighs, my sex gripping the one inside.

"Go slow." He squeezed my bottom with one big hand, the other working my clitoris—too many sensations at once. The pressure forced a sharper angle, and I felt him drag along a place that made my toes curl against his calves.

"Oh God—oh shit. I can't call you that, can I?"

"Just don't call me late for dinner." The bed creaked under his massive weight, and he chuckled—a happy rumble as his cock throbbed, and then jerked, tantalizing every tissue.

"Don't make me laugh, handsome man. And besides, I'm a terrible cook." I sank deeper, taking more of him.

"I will look after you." He ran his fingers down my spine, his eyes shifting hue as they met mine.

"Why me?" I whimpered, my heart shattered for this being—the one who waited for me alone, century after century.

"You are my love. My life. If I spend inside of you, you will see our past, but this knowledge comes with risk." His voice shadowed with concern.

"I want to come with you. I want to see." I fell into him, taking his lips, sucking each one into my mouth, licking his tongue, tasting something forbidden.

"You're so fucking hot." His fingertips pressed into my

bottom, filling me with hunger, a lust I had never felt before.

"Rurik, you swore. You said 'fuck.' What else can you do with that dirty mouth of yours? Show me again." I slid against him, chasing the need. The slick glide of us made a soft sound that tightened something low in my stomach.

He tilted my face upward, kissing the soft skin under my jaw, holding my shoulder blades in the spread of his hands, and dropping close kisses over my sensitive skin. "You have no idea how I desire you."

The pull of his lips, the pressure of his hands, the sound of his voice. The air hummed between us.

"Cristabel." He thumbed my cheekbone, his gaze searching mine.

I looked into his mismatched eyes—and saw all that he hoped for. A moan escaped my lips.

"I can't hold out much longer." His cock flexed inside me, tightening with each breath. He rolled his hips upward, finding a rhythm that made my spine bow. "I burn for you."

"Oh fuck. Oh, shit, fucking Christ. You did this to me." My need quickened, my nerves lit and humming.

Lightning tore through the sky. The pressure crested so suddenly I couldn't brace for it. My thighs shook. My stomach tightened in a sharp, rolling pull I couldn't stop. I threw my head back as pleasure broke through me in a blinding rush, my vision going soft at the edges.

"You are mine. And I am yours." He pressed his lips along the side of my face, his voice filled with conviction.

"I didn't think I could feel this." My body gripped him hard. Still, Rurik did not come.

"What do I make you feel?" He looked at me, face to face, nose to nose, his need raw and visible.

"Safe. Happy. I could stay here forever."

"Then you will stay." His fingers skated over my heated flesh, his lips nibbling the shell of my ear.

I pressed my lips against his, barely containing my smile. "You haven't come, Rurik. I'm waiting for the big reveal. What's behind door number two?"

"Funny. Funny girl." He suckled the nape of my neck, his cock throbbing inside me.

I arched into him, my nails dragging down his shoulders.

He slowed suddenly, lifting my hips, pulling almost all the way out. The absence made me gasp.

His forehead pressed to mine.

"I don't want to lose you," he murmured, his words soft.

The vulnerability in that admission hit harder than any thrust.

"I'm not leaving," I whispered. Not breathless. Not uncertain.

His fingers dug into my hips.

That was the moment he let go.

"I NEED to claim you the old way."

"The old way? You mean doggy style?" I cupped his face and licked his mouth.

His scent captivated me. Cold wind. Dark shadows. He was flesh and bone, but so much more. Anticipation made me want.

"My seed will carry memory. Not just pleasure. You will see what we were. What we lost."

He wasn't asking for obedience.

He was asking if I wanted truth.

"I want it."

A thrill ran through me.

"I'm shaking for you, Viking boy." I needed what he promised. "Show me."

He lifted me from him slowly, watching my face as he did it—as if he needed proof I wasn't vanishing.

When he laid me on the bed, I stretched willingly, raising my arms above my head. My breasts pressed into the mattress. Need gathered low and heavy between my thighs.

When he knelt behind me, the air shifted.

His fingers slid down my spine, tracing patterns that made my muscles tremble. When he spread my knees wider, I didn't feel exposed. I felt chosen.

"Don't be afraid."

"I'm not."

And I wasn't.

When his mouth touched me there, my hips bucked forward. His tongue moved with patient intensity, tasting slowly, drawing soft, deliberate strokes that made my hips roll helplessly toward him.

The pleasure spread slow and heavy, stealing the strength from my arms.

By the time he positioned himself behind me again, I was shaking—not from uncertainty—but from wanting him to stop holding back.

The first thrust pushed into me with a fullness that made my breath catch.

Not rough—inevitable.

He filled me completely, chest against my back, one hand braced beside my head, the other gripping my hip as if anchoring himself to this moment in time.

He didn't move at first. He stayed there, fully inside me, breathing with me, letting the stretch settle.

Then he began to move. And the pace was no longer careful. It was decisive.

"Oooh, yes. Oh, Rurik." My core clenched, and my clitoris ached. My fingertips brushed the carved runes. His second thrust dragged against something that made my thighs shake.

"My love. My one." He shuddered and lost himself, his shaft sweeping deep, striking something I hadn't known was waiting.

"More. Harder." I lost my mind in him. I fell over the edge with him.

"Cristabel." He roared my name, gliding into me, surrendering to his need.

The tension coiled fast this time—without hesitation. His thrusts grew harder, enough to steal my breath.

Pleasure broke through me, tearing a cry from my throat as my muscles spasmed around him.

I heard the rough break in his breath. "Cristabel—"

He thrust once more, forcing a sound from me I didn't recognize, and something deep inside me turned. It didn't snap. It turned—like a key settling fully into place. His release wasn't just physical. It was force. It spilled into me and struck something already stirring.

My heart stuttered hard against my ribs.

Rurik went rigid, arms locking around me—not in ecstasy, but in readiness.

He was waiting for the answer.

Then it resumed—stronger.

I knew the moment he realized. I was still breathing. Something older moved through me, steady and undeniable. Energy surged—then drew tight. When he stilled, everything around us held.

For a split second—the crackle of the hearth, the creak of the bed, even our ragged breathing—stilled. My heartbeat hammered.

Light ripped outward from where we joined, racing through my veins, up my spine, into my skull. The vines beneath my scars flared, searing a pattern I couldn't see but somehow knew—flaring bright enough to hurt—and somewhere deep beneath the world, a voice answered.

Awaken, little star.

It wasn't a command.

It was confirmation.

And somewhere deep beneath stone and root, something shifted in its sleep.

Rurik felt it too—I knew he did.

Whatever had spoken was sure of me.

My breath left me. Who…?

But the voice vanished, leaving only Rurik's hands, only light.

The ceiling dissolved into night. Above us, not in the room but through it, the great tree rose again—vaster, clearer than ever before. Branches reached into a sky streaked with aurora. Roots plunged into darkness. Runes glowed like living script along the trunk.

Threads of light streamed from my chest toward the tree and into the bark. I wasn't being taken. I was being *recognized*. Images slammed into me—too fast to hold.

A longship cut through black water, spray stinging my face as Rurik laughed at the prow.

A candlelit studio, my hands stained with ink as I drew a silver-haired Valkyrie and signed the name Cadence.

A Paris street, a stolen kiss under a flickering lamppost.

A hospital bed, the steady beep of a machine.

And the most painful one—Rurik's unseen presence pressed against my soul as I whispered, *I'm not ready to go.* Life. Death. Life again. Always him.

The pain of every ending was still there—but it no longer owned me.

I waited for the weakness.

For that subtle unravelling—something inside me beginning to let go.

It didn't come.

Rurik felt it too. His arms tightened around me—not in relief, but in something guarded. As if he had braced for a change in me that never arrived.

I hadn't thinned. I hadn't broken.

The tree held us both—every version of me, every version of him—threads crossing and severing and crossing again.

This was always the moment when something in me would begin to fade. When joy would carry an edge of ending. When time would feel shorter without either of us knowing why. But I did not feel smaller or fragile. I felt present.

"Do you see it?" His voice was rough.

"Everything," I whispered. "I see everything."

The tree's light dimmed. The runes cooled beneath my fingertips. Pine walls returned. Firelight steadied. His weight remained wrapped around me. But the space inside my chest—the place that had always felt borrowed—did not hollow.

It stayed full.

The stillness that followed was different—not empty, not ending. I didn't know what staying would cost. Only that leaving had always cost more.

27

WHAT LOOKED BACK

Cristabel

The certainty settled deep and calm, nothing like the rush that had brought it. As if a presence that had always been there was finally recognized.

Whatever storms waited beyond this night, I knew one thing: I wasn't alone anymore. And neither was he.

"Are you all right?" He lay over me, his breath heavy, his heart pounding in his chest, and his cock thrumming inside me.

"I'm wonderful."

He exhaled against my neck—relief and hunger tangled together—then rolled his hips, testing the way my body welcomed him.

I arched instinctively.

He groaned—low and reverent.

"Say it again."

His hands slid down my thighs, spreading me wider beneath him. He didn't thrust. He pressed, letting me feel every inch of him.

"I'm wonderful," I breathed, and the second time it wasn't reassurance. It felt different.

He drove deeper.

Slow at first. Then fuller. The stretch of him made my breath stutter, made my hips lift to meet him. I felt every inch as he withdrew and pressed back in, not hurried, not gentle—intent.

"Are you crying?" I touched his face, the soft skin around his eyes.

"No." He smiled, his eyes glittering, then he kissed the top of my nose.

"You are crying. Why are you crying?" I clasped his angled jaw, pulling his mouth to mine.

"Because I'm happy. You make me happy." The word *happy* sounded unfamiliar in his mouth. He wrapped his arms around me.

"What are you?" I leaned into him. "You're made of flesh and bone. You feel like a man, but you're more than that. If I rub my eyes, will you disappear? Is this just a wonderful dream? A fairy tale?"

"I would settle for the hero in your fairy tale. I would like that very much." He shifted, spooning me with his entire body.

"My hero? That's shallow, isn't it?" I snuggled into him, his leg wrapped over mine.

"Perhaps…but for now, it is enough." The words *for now* carried weight. Heroes always came with endings. He kissed my cheekbone, the palm of his hand resting between my legs.

"For now?" I pressed into him, aching.

He answered by shifting his hips, sliding forward until the head of him dragged exactly where I needed it. My back arched. My nails dug into his forearm. The ache sharpened into something brighter.

"I will spend eternity making you fall in love with me." His fingertips stroked my sex, the weight of his hips heavy on mine.

"I love you already, Viking boy. You know that." I cuddled into him, resting my head in the crook of his shoulder. "Tell me about the runes on the headboard. They came to life when I touched them."

"Does that scare you?" His cock jerked, wanting more.

"Why do you keep asking if I'm afraid?" I closed my eyes and pressed, gasping as he filled me again, and again.

"It's not easy to explain to a human the existence of other beings. Most would lose their balance. Perhaps break down. But you're taking this quite well." His chest rumbled deep. His hand slid between my thighs, fingers finding the slick heat there, circling, pressing, learning the rhythm my body was already begging for.

"Other beings? What kind?" I rested my hands over his, rocking with him, the crescendo rising.

"Elves. Giants." His rhythm slowed, at one with mine.

Then he changed it. Shorter strokes. Deeper. The kind that made my toes curl and my breath catch in helpless little sounds I couldn't swallow back.

"Elves?" I huffed a small, breathless laugh. "Like Lord of the Rings elves?"

The word should have sounded absurd. Instead, it slid into place like something I had once known and buried.

"I remember the stairwell." My breath hitched as he drove into me again. "The limousine."

With one hand, he cupped my breasts, his thumb brushing my nipples. The sensation shot straight down, tightening everything low in my belly. My hips rocked harder, chasing him. Every touch made my thighs tremble.

"The hotel in Barcelona."

Each memory struck sharp and undeniable—like my body had been waiting for permission to open.

Different names. Different cities. Same mouth. Same hands.

My body clenched around him, hard, and his control faltered. He swore under his breath and thrust into me again, deeper than before, holding me there as his thumb pressed firm, deliberate circles.

The pressure built fast—too fast. My thighs trembled. My spine arched.

"Rurik—" I didn't finish. I couldn't.

The release hit sharp and blinding, tearing through me in waves that stole my breath and left my muscles pulsing around him.

The runes along the headboard flared faintly behind us.

Not fantasy. Memory.

"I remember the taste of your sweet nectar on my lips." His warmth skittered across my skin.

"Life after death. So, it's real." The words felt too small for the truth pressing in around me. A flicker moved behind my eyes—

Astrid with frost in her lashes.

Edda standing in a torchlit hall.

Cadence reaching for me through smoke.

Three women. Three shadows wearing my face.

All waiting for me to remember. Not to reclaim them. To acknowledge they had happened.

"You will always be my thing. The woman I love. The

woman I want." He kissed the corners of my mouth and then chased my tongue, all the while gliding deeper.

He followed me over the edge, thrusting once—twice—before going still inside me with a rough groan against my throat. His weight settled heavy and real, his breath breaking against my skin while he held himself there, neither of us trusting the moment to last.

We didn't move right away. He stayed inside me, softening slowly, his hand still curved between my thighs. My fingers traced the line of his shoulder, the scar near his collarbone, the steady rise and fall of his chest.

Our breathing settled into the same rhythm—in, out, in, out.

The world narrowed to skin and air and the quiet thud of his heart beneath my palm.

Sleep tugged at me in warm, lazy waves, but beneath the cabin a vibration stirred, too faint to be real.

I turned onto my side. Rurik breathed steadily beside me, one arm heavy across my waist. I closed my eyes.

...Beloved...

I jerked awake. The voice wasn't a sound. It was a brush of cold thought across my mind—soft as moth wings, ancient as winter.

You burn.

The thought held no warmth.

The phrasing bothered me—not the warning, but the assumption.

My vines pulsed beneath my ribs, once. I sat up, heart pounding. "Rurik... did you hear... "

He did not move.

His breathing stayed slow.

The silence returned so completely that I questioned

my sanity. Just a dream, I told myself. Jet lag. Adrenaline. Too much sex and not enough sleep.

The vines glowed faintly under my skin a moment longer, like an unseen presence had brushed against it.

The warmth faded reluctantly, as though whatever listened hadn't expected me to answer.

Rurik

Cristabel slept draped over me, soft as a midsummer breeze, her breath fanning across my chest. I did not move. Even the smallest shift felt like a risk—like reminding the world she was here.

In other lives, I had felt it begin within hours of her remembering—an invisible tightening in the air, as if time itself had marked her for retrieval. It was never dramatic. It was worse than that—gradual. A sense that something unseen had already started counting down.

There was no counting now.

Sleep was a luxury for men who believed morning was guaranteed.

The room was dark except for the faint glow of her vines—those delicate, living tendrils pulsing beneath her skin with a rhythm not entirely mortal. I had seen that light before, and each time it had been followed by the narrowing. She had never noticed it. Mortals rarely did when the extraordinary rose from within their own bodies.

I had learned not to name it too soon. Not to press too hard. Wonder could turn to fear quickly, and fear to distance. That ignorance had preserved her more than once.

I held her as if memory itself were fragile.

What we had done—what she had become—should have frightened me. In previous lifetimes, awakening came with strain, with rupture, with consequence already gathering at the edges of the world.

This time, she had opened herself willingly.

That was the difference.

Her soul—old and bright—had risen because she chose to remember.

A creak moved through the cabin floor. It was not wood or wind. It was earth. The vibration traveled up through the bedposts and into my ribs—an ancient pulse I had known across centuries. My body recognized it before thought caught up.

The tunnels were stirring beneath us.

They had stirred before, but never like this. Her awakening had always carried a cost, and that cost had claimed her before anything beneath the mountain had the chance to rise fully. She would remember. She would burn brighter. And then she would fade. The fire had never been allowed to anchor.

Now it had.

I did not speak the name of what lived below. I knew the sound by heart. I had heard it beneath stone halls and timber homes, beneath cities long erased.

It had felt her awakening—and it had felt that she remained.

The curse had always taken her swiftly once memory returned, as though the world could not tolerate her holding both love and knowledge at once. I had learned to recognize the moment the closing began. I searched for it now.

There was nothing.

The absence unsettled me more than any roar.

A low sound moved through the mountain. Not hunger. Not rage.

It knew her.

It wanted her.

Hope was worse than hunger. Hunger could be fed. Hope lingered.

The presence below brushed the edges of my mind, patient as ever.

I tightened my arms around her sleeping form. "No. You will not have her."

The mountain shifted in answer, remembering me as well.

Cristabel stirred, nuzzling closer, unaware of the ancient patience coiling beneath us.

In other lifetimes, I had felt time fold inward the moment she awakened. Breath shortened. Luck thinned. Fate began its quiet harvest.

The air did not fold now.

I did not mistake that for mercy. The cycle that once protected the world by taking her early had failed to close. Her death had always been enough to seal what lay beneath us for another span of years.

But if she no longer died when she awakened—if the fire remained rooted in living flesh—then the old restraint would not hold.

The darkness below did not surge. It did not need to. It had been waiting for this moment far longer than I had.

That unsettled me more than rage ever had.

Something in her had changed. She was no longer only returning. She was taking root.

A pressure tightened beneath my ribs—not desire, not anger, but memory.

The thing beneath Røros had many names. None would be spoken tonight. Across centuries, one truth had endured: it desired what it could never keep.

I understood that too well.

I had lived centuries wanting what time denied me.

I bent and kissed the crown of Cristabel's head, breathing her in. Her vines glowed once beneath my palm, then dimmed.

She was safe—for now.

For now was all eternity had ever given me.

Far below, something ancient coiled upon itself, restless and aware that it was no longer contained.

In every life before, this was the hour she began to slip from me—the subtle unravelling neither of us could prevent once it began. Her breathing remained steady. Her pulse was strong beneath my hand.

The world had not claimed her.

And because it had not, something older would try.

28

THE MORNING AFTER THE MOON

C*ristabel*

The new moon cast a glassy shadow, the sun hidden by the rest of the planet. In this land of polar night, a blue haze bathed the bedroom. Time felt suspended here, as if morning had stalled at the horizon. I couldn't tell whether hours or moments had passed—only that the world hadn't rushed in to reclaim me.

Odin stood on top of me, kneading his front paws into my chest, chirping low-pitched trills, and pressing his face into mine. His purr vibrated straight through my ribs, steady and insistent, like he was anchoring me to the bed.

"What's wrong, bud? What are you trying to tell me?" I rubbed both sides of his furry face and gazed into his single blue eye.

He jumped to the floor, slipping behind a carved door and vanishing into a closet. The door didn't quite close behind him. It lingered open, just enough to make me feel watched rather than alone. Not threatened. Observed. In that moment, he wasn't a pet. He felt like a witness. Like he had been watching me longer than this life.

The kettle whistled from the kitchen below, and the aroma of baking bread drifted up into the upstairs loft. I rolled over in the big bed and held Rurik's pillow in my arms, breathing in his scent. Woodsmoke. Cold air. Something darker beneath it, like stone warmed by fire. My body reacted before my thoughts did.

Something old stirred beneath my heartbeat, as if a thread tugged gently from a life I hadn't lived in this body.

Not a memory—a return. Not to a place. To a way of standing in the world I didn't yet understand. The sensation didn't rush me. It settled, careful and patient, like something that had learned not to scare me away. I had the strange sense that if I stayed still long enough, it would finish unfolding on its own.

I should have been afraid. Relief unsettled me more.

Instead, I felt steadier than I had in years, as if last night I'd stepped into the skin that always belonged to me. Not younger. Not stronger. Just truer. As if I'd finally stopped pretending to be someone passing through my own life.

My body longed for him. My heart yearned for him.

Odin meowed from inside the closet, engaging in a game of cat and mouse. His voice wasn't demanding. It was insistent in a way that felt purposeful, like he was nudging me toward something he'd already decided I needed to see.

I followed the cat into a closet the size of a small bedroom, where I discovered fashions from a different era. I ran my fingers over fine weaves and silky fabrics.

Dresses. Mine. My hands knew where to go before my eyes did. I traced seams, hems, closures—movements so familiar they made my throat tighten. I didn't remember choosing these clothes. I remembered *wearing* them—and being chosen in them.

Choking back a sob, I pressed my nose to a navy velvet gown, drawn to the scent rising from the antique material. Not perfume. Not age. Something human. Something worn often enough to remember its owner. What about next time? Would he find me again? The thought landed heavier than it should have. I realized I wasn't thinking about leaving.

One dress caught my eye—a heavy linen weave, narrow at the waist with flounced sleeves, adorned with intricate embroidery. I took the dress off the hanger and stood in front of the mirror, a vision of a church wedding from long ago drifting through my mind, and the sound of violin strings guiding me down the long nave toward Rurik—his hands clasped, waiting for me. The memory carried weight—the ache of anticipation, the steadiness of commitment—not the rush of romance. Whatever this had been, it hadn't been impulsive. It had been decided. The image didn't fade when I blinked. It held.

Odin meowed, a precocious grin on his furry face. He looked unbearably pleased with himself, like he'd just delivered a message I wasn't ready to receive.

"What are you trying to tell me, Odin?" He rubbed against my legs, then disappeared again.

Dress shirts hung from the shortest bar, trousers from another. Shelves rose to the ceiling, stacked neatly with white, black, and grey T-shirts. Everything was as it should be. I was home. The certainty startled me. I'd never thought of myself as someone who belonged easily anywhere. Belonging, I was learning, wasn't about permission. It was about being known.

I pulled on a white T-shirt over my head and giggled at my reflection in the oval mirror — the hem reached past my knees, and my face was flushed with a rosy pink. I looked softer like this. Less guarded. Like someone who expected to be loved when she walked into a room—and not braced to leave. The thought startled me with its gentleness. I'd spent years armouring myself against disappointment. Somewhere along the line, I'd forgotten how to expect joy.

I padded down the glass steps, unable to quiet my rising need. It wasn't just hunger. It was certainty—my body expecting him to be exactly where he was. Each step felt preordained, my feet moving with the certainty of habit rather than choice.

Everything in the great room was just as we left it the night before—logs crackled in the stone fireplace, candles flickered on every surface. The Christmas tree sparkled with white lights. Nothing had reset while I slept. No illusion broken. No spell undone. If magic had touched this place, it hadn't disrupted it. It had *settled in*.

My gaze settled on the oak dais and the massive floor pillow, thoughts of the evening's pleasure rushing through my mind in a frantic need. My thighs tightened reflexively. The memory lived in my body, not my head. I wondered how many truths I'd carried like that—felt before they were named.

"God Jul, my princess. How are you feeling this morning?" Rurik, clothed in loose-fitting gray sweats and a form-fitting white T-shirt, his muscles flexing with delectable definition, stood, his head bent over a blueberry-coloured cast-iron pot, stirring the ingredients with a long wooden spoon.

The sight of him like this—grounded, unhurried—felt more intimate than the night before. Desire was easy. This—this quiet normalcy wrapped around something extraordinary—felt like trust.

"What are you making?" My stomach grumbled, enticed by the man before me.

"Risengrynsgrøt, a Christmas Eve tradition." He lifted the spoon toward my mouth. "Taste."

He watched me closely as I swallowed, like the act itself mattered. I had the odd impression I was being welcomed, not just fed.

"Hmm…it's good." I closed my eyes, savouring the flavours of rice and butter.

His eyes warmed as he ladled spoonfuls into an earthenware bowl, then dropped a skinned almond on top. Something about the gesture felt deliberate, ceremonial, even if he treated it lightly. The almond sat there like a secret, unremarkable to anyone who didn't know what to look for.

"Is that for me?" I saddled up behind him, pressing into his warmth.

"Uh, uh. Nope, this is for the Nisse." He topped off the porridge with a sprinkle of cinnamon and a dollop of creamy butter.

"The Nisse? The little man with the pointy hat? Are you telling me you believe that fairy tale? You do, don't you?" I dropped my hand under the waistband of his grey sweats, groping for morning wood.

"We must keep the Nisse happy, or bad things will come." He said it playfully—but not dismissively. Like someone repeating a rule they'd learned the hard way. The way he said it made me think of old bargains—of forces that didn't disappear just because you'd survived them. Belief wasn't the point. Respect was.

His grin told me that all things were possible. I wanted answers. I wanted him more.

"What bad things?" I pulled the drawstring around his waist with my other hand.

"Come. I have a surprise for you." The word *surprise* stirred something beneath my ribs. Not urgency—expectation. I was beginning to understand that here, the way he waited wasn't passive. It was an act of faith.

He kissed my forehead, leaving the kitchen with the Nisse's bowl of porridge. He didn't lead me far—just beyond the main room, through a low doorway I hadn't noticed before. The air changed immediately. Cooler. Sharper.

Shelves lined the walls, rough-hewn but carefully tended. Not storage—*curation*. Objects placed with intention.

I slowed, my pulse ticking louder in my ears.

"This isn't…?"

He shook his head.

"Not yet."

He stepped closer, not touching me—just close enough that I felt the heat of him along my side.

My gaze moved over the shelves again.

Not antiques. Not relics. Things worn smooth by hands that had known them well.

My throat closed—not with fear. With familiarity.

Like standing in a room I had once known in the dark.

He didn't guide me forward. He didn't reach for anything.

He waited.

And somehow that waiting felt more intimate than if he had taken my hand.

I exhaled slowly.

"Another time," I murmured.

His mouth curved, just slightly.

As we crossed back into the main room, I paused.

The fire burned lower than it should have. Not dying—*watchful*. As if conserving itself.

Something in the room had shifted—not broken. Adjusted.

Rurik noticed my hesitation but didn't comment. His hand found mine, warm and steady, grounding me again.

Whatever I'd felt slipped just out of reach. But the impression lingered—like the air before a storm you couldn't yet see.

When he stepped away for a moment, I pressed my palm to my chest.

The familiar ache was gone.

I stilled.

For years, I had carried something small and sharp beneath everything—a quiet readiness for impact, a habit of tightening before joy could settle. It wasn't dramatic. It just lived there.

I reached for my chest once more.

Nothing tightened back.

The absence didn't feel like relief.

It felt… open.

As if some internal brace I'd forgotten I was holding had finally released.

Whatever he was leading me toward felt inevitable—like turning a page I'd written long ago.

29

THE BARN OF OLD SOULS

Cristabel

"Where are you taking the porridge?" I trailed after him, my body aching for him.

"The barn, for the Nisse." He lifted an eyebrow and grinned, then handed me a snowsuit hanging on a hook by the door.

"The barn? You make the Nisse eat in the barn? Maybe a hungry mouse is eating your porridge."

I slid into the neon pink onesie—a perfect fit. The question hovered on my tongue, and then I realized that in some other life, this was mine. All these things were mine, and Rurik saved them for my return.

Recognition moved through me—like muscle memory, but deeper. The more I took in, the more it felt unfinished.

The porch floorboards creaked, frosted from the cold night. The bitter wind stung my cheeks. We followed the moonbeam toward the red barn—the courtyard dusted with snow. My boots crunched with each step, but Rurik moved silently.

Shivers raced down my spine, and the hairs on my nape rose. There was a presence about this place. Would I ever get used to it? I giggled when Odin raced ahead.

For a while, the world behaved.

Sound settled into its proper places—boots on snow, breath clouding the air, the small ordinary rhythms of life continuing without interruption. I let myself believe it.

"Come on, before you catch your death." He slid the barn door open with one hand—a kissable grin on his otherworldly face, the bowl of porridge balanced in his other hand.

I stopped in the snow, my mind chasing those words. *Death.* I would die one day, and he wouldn't. I couldn't unsee it.

"Princess?" His voice reached me, his forehead creased into three distinct lines.

My heart clenched thinking of the slumbering dead and whether they would rise again. I wanted to cry. But even as fear gripped my chest, a deeper, older voice answered.

Not with words. Just a steadiness beneath my ribs. The fear didn't take root.

"I'm sorry. I shouldn't have said that. I wasn't thinking." In that moment, he was so human, so flawed. I loved him more.

Sweet-smelling hay and that horsey aroma surrounded us. Caged lanterns hung from the barn board ceiling, and a ladder led up into the hayloft. Oversized box stalls lined each side of the wide hallway—nothing out of place. So Rurik. So Nisse.

The sound inside the barn felt stretched—like a held note pulled too tight.

He placed the porridge on a sparkling workbench inside a tack room, filled with polished leather, breast-plates, bridles, and harnesses.

Odin ghosted past on the rubber-tiled floor, in a blur of shadow and light.

From behind the bars of a large box stall, a black stallion nickered—his magnificent mane flowing over a sculpted neck and, in the neighbouring stall, a white mare.

"I know this horse." I gasped, pulled toward the horse by an unseen thread. I left Rurik and stepped into the mare's stall. She stood on a thick bed of straw, her belly heavy with foal, her unblinking blue eyes fixed on me. I reached out and brushed my hand over her rounded belly.

Warmth bloomed beneath my palm. The sensation travelled deeper than skin—down my arm, through my spine, into the place where standing becomes belonging. I had the strange thought that the ground itself knew me.

"Yes, you do." His dimples etched his cheeks, and laugh lines fanned out from his eyes.

"Moon," I whispered her name, and her ears flickered in recognition. "Her teats are waxing. She's due any day."

"She is. This is her first foal." He leaned against the door frame, looking at the mare with affection.

"Really? Why?" I gazed at the stallion and the healthy mare, my thoughts scattered.

"Immortals don't often birth here." His gaze filled with light, and he reached for my hand, pulling me into his embrace. "Sometimes miracles happen."

The quiet beneath my scars answered him—not flaring, not burning. Just… present. Like a breath drawn and not yet released.

"Hmm… Let's get back to this immortal thing?" I

shook my head, realizing he was right—he was oh so right. How many times had I come back? "How many immortals are there?"

The air shifted.

"More than you think." He lifted me onto a bale of straw—towering over me—not so much.

"What's the plan? A little horseplay? Maybe a roll in the hay?" I rested my hands on his broad shoulders, catching his bottom lip and chasing his tongue.

"The better to kiss you with." He played along, skimming the inside of my mouth, feathering kisses over my cheekbones.

"Oh, are we role-playing? You're the big bad wolf, and I'm what? The girl with the snapdragon tattoo? That's quite the cosplay. Don't you think?" I wrapped my legs around his waist. I wanted him right there, right then.

"My plan is simple. Kissing you. Making love with you. Making you happy." He caged me against the rough barn board, deepening the kiss, stroking my tongue with his. Then he stopped. He planted one soft kiss on my nose.

"Rurik, don't stop now. You've made me hot." I moaned, breathing with him, my desire a need only he could answer.

"Have you forgotten the wedding? Your friend, Tiiná?" He gave me a sly grin and held my hands in his.

"The wedding? Shit fuck, goddamn. The wedding is today. How are we getting there?" My gaze darted to his.

He tilted his head toward the far end of the barn, where a shining red one-horse open sleigh waited. The black stallion tossed his head in the air, nickering in response.

"A sleigh ride? To the wedding?" The air flickered, and a vision of Rurik and me in wedding attire flashed through my mind. "How many times have we been together?"

Rurik's expression softened, something ancient flickering through his mismatched eyes.

Images flickered behind my ribs—braids and battle-smoke, ink-stained fingers, a candlelit room where someone whispered my name—echoes, not memories.

"We always meet in the middle of a storm." He lifted my hand to his lips. "Different centuries. Different body. Same soul. Same you."

The kiss he pressed to my knuckles was reverent, almost trembling.

"And when I die?" I asked. "You still love me?" I leaned my forehead against his, my breath hitching.

"You are the air I breathe. There will never be another." He brushed his lips across my cheekbones, fingers threading through my hair as if re-learning me, as if memorizing me again.

Something in me eased. Not breaking. Not bracing. Just… shared.

"We should hurry, my love. The elf awaits." He lifted me onto my feet, turning away with a smile.

"The elf?" My hair lifted as if caught in a breeze. "What elf?"

The wind shifted outside the barn. As he led away, a faint pulse stirred beneath my ribs—warm, certain, alive.

My vines whispered against my skin, answering something I could not yet hear.

Whatever waited beyond this moment, I knew one thing:

I wasn't walking toward it alone.

Far beneath the quiet of snow and timber, something ancient stirred—aware now that this time, I had chosen to stay.

EPILOGUE

In the deep places where roots drink silence,
I remain.
Stone is my cradle.
The dark, my crown.
A king unremembered—
still remembering.
Her fire did not fade.
Her thread holds.
The pattern alters.
He will go to her.
He always does.
The last time, I slept through the breaking.
This time—
I will be awake.
—Eldvarr, King-Below

CONTINUE THE STORY IN FIREVEIN: THE TAKING

COMING SOON

HANNA PARK

1

HE WAS ALREADY THERE

C*ristabel*

The runners whispered over tracked snow, the world narrowing to breath, rhythm, and the steady, unhurried pull of the horse before us.

Pale light filtered through the trees, catching on the frost without warmth.

Cold bit at my cheeks, but the blanket around my legs still held his warmth—solid, real, familiar in a way that no longer startled.

A lightness settled in me—unexpected—as though I had stopped fighting what I already knew.

"Tiinná's an elf." The words came easily, which bothered me. I tipped my head slightly, catching the difference in his eyes again, as though they never quite agreed on what they were seeing. "Do I get a guidebook, Viking boy, or am I figuring this out as we go?"

His arm tightened around me, not quite a laugh, not relaxed either. "You're managing."

"Good," I murmured, adjusting the edge of the blanket

with one hand. "Because I feel like I missed a very important orientation session."

The sleigh carried us forward, the trees thinning as the road opened toward town. For a moment, nothing moved beyond my sight.

By the time the sleigh reached the church, the town was already awake, though the market itself was quiet.

The stalls stood closed along the main square, their wooden fronts latched and dark, a dusting of snow blurring their edges. Beyond them, a tall spruce rose at the center, its branches heavy with frost and strung lights not yet lit, the skating ring circling it smooth and pale, marked only by the faint tracks of someone who had been there before dawn.

Ice candles flickered low along the doorsteps of the narrow houses, their flames small but steady inside carved hollows, catching against painted wood where snow had gathered. Smoke drifted lazily from chimneys, the scent of it mixing with something sweet and spiced that lingered in the cold.

An orange cat slipped between two doorways, tail high, pausing just long enough to watch me, not the sleigh, not the street, before slipping out of sight.

Farther off came the low, distant sound of the train easing into the station, metal against metal cutting through cold air.

The church bells followed a moment later, low and resolute, their sound rolling out across the square. They should have faded. Instead, the last note lingered a fraction too long—caught, as if it had found somewhere to stay.

Then it shifted.

Not the road. Not the horse. Something beneath it.

The rhythm didn't stop, but it slipped just enough that it ran through my spine before I understood it. The horse's ears flicked back, its gait hitching for a step before smoothing out again.

I stilled, my hand tightening in the folds of the blanket. "Did you feel that?"

Rurik didn't answer. His hand stayed at my waist, not pulling me closer, just holding.

"I felt something," I added, softer now, listening in a way that had nothing to do with sound.

It brushed me again before I could name it, not a voice, not a thought, but close enough that my breath caught.

Beloved.

I straightened on the bench seat, scanning the dark between the trees. Nothing moved. Nothing answered.

I exhaled, the sound almost a quiet laugh. "All right," I murmured. "We're doing that now, apparently."

I leaned back into him anyway—closer, warmer. It didn't silence anything.

The horse stamped, then stamped again, its ears flicking toward the ground more than the crowd.

Rurik leaned forward, tightening the reins as the horse shifted in the traces, the harness creaking softly with the movement. "Easy."

The word was enough.

The animal settled only partway.

"You feel it." His gaze remained ahead.

I turned toward him, the lace at my wrist shifting as I moved, the edge of it sliding back just enough to reveal the ink beneath.

The vines traced upward along my skin in fine, curling

lines, the same pattern I had chosen to cover what had once been taken from me, delicate enough to pass for ornament if you didn't look closely.

They didn't feel like ornament now.

The pull came from beneath the skin, just enough to make my fingers curl against the fabric, not pain, not quite movement, but something that answered.

"I feel something. It isn't the town."

His attention dropped immediately. He took my wrist and pulled the sleeve back. exposing the ink fully, his thumb pressing into one of the dark curves, testing it—expecting it to answer.

"It's gone further." His jaw tightened as he traced the line.

I watched his hand, the way it lingered there. "You've seen this before."

His thumb shifted slightly, more deliberate.

It moved beneath us.

Not the sleigh, not the horse—deeper. The cold didn't change, but it reached me, a slow warmth threading upward through the packed snow—too deliberate to be anything natural.

My vines responded at once, drawing tight beneath my skin, the pull deeper now, harder to ignore. Not reacting. They were answering.

His thumb remained there, the pressure unyielding.

"It was never meant to reach this point." His voice dropped, edged sharper. "It ends before this. It always has."

The words settled between us, carrying the weight of something that had never failed.

But the lines on my skin didn't fade. I watched them,

my breath catching as the pull intensified. I could no longer pretend.

"I didn't end." My voice lowered—quieter than I intended, but just as firm as the lines marking my skin.

I didn't look away when I said it.

His grip closed around mine, not correcting me, not agreeing, as if that was the only part of this he trusted.

Behind us, the horse struck the ground sharply, the sound hollow enough to turn a few heads. A man near the steps looked over, his easy expression faltering as the animal failed to settle.

"Everything all right?"

Rurik didn't turn. "Fine."

He was already moving. The rest of the world rushed back in with it.

He stepped down from the sleigh and turned back at once, reaching for me again as I shifted toward the edge. His hand closed around mine, guiding me, while the other hovered at my waist as my boots found the snow.

The ground felt solid beneath me, though the movement I had sensed lingered deeper, out of reach.

Voices carried across the yard, laughter breaking easily between clusters of people gathered near the steps.

"God jul," someone called, the words warm and familiar as they passed, answered by the same in return.

The scent of spiced wine drifted through the cold—clove and orange, something sweet beneath it—catching low in the air where cups were passed between gloved hands.

A child ran past in a blur of red wool before being caught and turned back with a playful scold. Smoke lingered low between the buildings, softening the edges of everything as the church doors stood open, drawing people inside in a steady, unhurried flow.

People shifted as we approached, making space without breaking conversation.

Not for us.

Laughter carried on, but it didn't land the same way, a few voices trailing off as we passed.

A woman in deep green slowed at my side, her gaze catching on my wrist where the lace had slipped back, lingering a moment before lifting to my face, her expression smoothing too quickly.

Just beyond her, a man paused mid-step, his hand half-raised as if he had forgotten what he meant to do. He lowered it slowly, his gaze not on me, but just past me.

Near the doors, Tiinná stood among a cluster of women. I knew her at once—before I understood why. The blue of her dress caught first, deeper than anything else, the colour holding against the snow as if it belonged to something older than the day.

Silver flashed at her throat when she turned, not delicate, not meant to be.

She saw me, her expression opened, bright and easy in a way that should have settled everything.

It didn't.

"You made it."

Her gaze moved as she stepped closer, dropping briefly to my wrist before lifting again.

She drew me into an embrace before I could answer, holding for a breath longer than courtesy required.

"You look beautiful." The words were soft against my ear, but the way her hand pressed briefly at my wrist—testing.

Rurik stepped closer, narrowing the space between us, his hand steady on mine.

"The land decides nothing." His tone stayed even, but his grip tightened.

Tiinná brushed the edge of the doorframe beside her, her fingertips resting there as if feeling for something beneath the wood. Like she felt it too. When she looked back at me, the brightness hadn't left her, but it no longer reached her eyes.

"No. But it keeps what's given. And it knows when something comes back changed."

"I'm not returning."

Her gaze held mine, almost gentle.

"You already have."

The warmth surged again, deeper this time, as if something far below shifted.

Rurik sensed it.

"You crossed." Her gaze slipped past me, toward the open space beyond the doors. "And you brought something with you."

He didn't look at her.

"I know."

The bells began, low and full. Voices overlapped, laughter rising again as people turned toward the church, the steady flow of bodies moving through the open doors.

Rurik guided me forward, his body close enough that I could feel the tension in him with every step. I caught a glimpse toward the front—Lars standing near the altar, already waiting, his shoulders set, his attention shifting toward the entrance as people passed through.

Heat from the church pressed in, bringing with it the low murmur of voices as people settled into place. Movement continued in small shifts—fabric brushing, boots against wood, the quiet adjustment of bodies finding stillness.

Candlelight flickered along the walls, catching silver, catching eyes—things that didn't reflect the way they should. The colours shifted—deep blues and reds edged in intricate bands, the patterns repeating in ways that felt older than the building itself.

As we moved deeper into the church, something shifted. The heat no longer rose from beneath the ground. It gathered, threading through me toward what was already there.

I didn't have to search.

A man sat along the side wall, one arm stretched along the back of the bench, like he had every right to be there.

There was no sign of the cold on him. No damp. No melt.

The dark of his coat took the light instead of giving anything back. His hair fell just past his collar, unremarkable until you looked twice.

He looked young enough to belong among them.

He didn't.

People passed within arm's reach without looking directly at him, their paths shifting just enough to leave space where there should have been none.

Just behind him, closer to the wall, another figure stood, half in shadow, broader, unmoving—its stillness different. Less ease. More watchful.

I narrowed.

Rurik's attention followed mine, and then he stilled. Not stillness—recognition without a name. Like he was looking at something he had been taught never to see.

"No." A beat. "That's not—"

A breath left me before I could stop it.

"Right," I muttered. "Because this has all been perfectly normal."

A couple of heads turned.

Across the room, the man's attention didn't shift. It remained on me—the moment already in motion.

His gaze flicked. Not to the room. To Rurik. Not surprise. Not interest. Just a brief recognition—then dismissal.

Rurik saw it.

Not the man—where his attention rested. He understood, in that instant, that the presence across the room had already chosen its ground.

The warmth beneath my skin deepened, no longer distant, no longer contained.

Beside me, Rurik didn't move. Didn't speak. His jaw set in refusal. Something in him had already locked into place—as if the ground itself had shifted into a field he had been born to defend.

And for the first time since we had arrived, I understood—whatever moved beneath the ground had not followed me here.

It had been waiting for me.

ABOUT THE AUTHOR

Awards:

Resurrection

Imadjinn - Finalist - Fantasy Romance

The Scald Crow

Foreward Reviews - Finalist - Romance

Imadjinn - Finalist - Romance

CANREADS Book Award - Finalist - Fantasy

Literary Titan Book Award 2025

Readers' Choice Award 2025

Mary Christmas, a Steamy Small-town Romance.

N.N. Light's Book Heaven 2024 Book Awards

First Place for Best Holiday Romance

Unwrapped in Roros

Passionate Ink - 2023 Passionate Plume - Finalist

Finding Tiegan

American Book Fest Awards 2023

Winner - Romance Erotica

Paranormal Romance Guild

Second Place 2022 Reviewer &

Reader Choice Award

Contemporary Romance Writers

Stiletto Contest Winner 2022

N.N. Lights Book Award 2021

Best Erotic Romance

Sorrento Seduction

Passionate Ink - 2022 Passionate Plume - Finalist

N.N. Lights Book Award 2022 - Finalist

Hanna's Story:

I began my writing career in the pre-dawn of a winter morning while my husband snored like a train. We could call my husband the catalyst. If not for him, I would never have gone to the kitchen to make coffee, feed the cat, and sit on the loveseat in front of the fire. In those moments of wondrous quiet, it was there that I did something I had never thought possible. I opened my laptop, and while the coffee went cold, I wrote a story. My husband had no idea that these sojourns to the loveseat in front of the fire would become a daily occurrence, that writing would become an obsession, but the cat knew. She knows everything.

I write stories that make you laugh, make you cry, and make you love. Thank you, friends, for reading!

In the beginning, there was an empty page.

I am a writer who lives in Muskoka, Canada, with a husband who snores, a hungry cat, and an almost perfect canine—he's an adorable little shit.

Visit Hanna Park at

https://www.hannapark.ca

ALSO BY HANNA PARK

Novels

The Scald Crow, Beyond the Faerie Rath, Book 1

Resurrection, Beyond the Faerie Rath, Book 2

Tides of Treacher, Beyond the Faerie Rath, Book 3 - COMING SOON

Finding Tiegan

Novellas

Mary Christmas

Unwrapped in Roros

Sorrento Seduction

Made in United States
Cleveland, OH
01 June 2026

37609667R00160